Tales from the CANYONS of the DAMNED

PRESENTED BY USA TODAY BESTSELLING AUTHOR
DANIEL ARTHUR SMITH

Tales from the Canyons of the Damned 42

Special thanks to editor Jessica West

  First Edition ISBN: 978-1-946777-85-0

Cover By Daniel Arthur Smith

Horror Fiction from Holt Smith ltd
Agroland
Tower
Attack of the Kung Fu Mummies

For Susan, Tristan, & Oliver, as all things are.

Worth a Thousand Screams

Robert Jeschonek

Sunday, October 30, 1983, 10:00 P.M.

When I think of my favorite weekend activities, staring at the obliterated corpse of a fellow member of the photojournalistic profession does *not* come to mind.

Yet that is exactly what I find myself doing on this particular Sunday night, taking in the terrible view in a dilapidated tenement room alongside a number of Pittsburgh, Pennsylvania's so-called finest. All over the grimy floor—and walls, and ceiling—are the remains of one Sylvester "Sylver" Seaver, a news photographer considered one of the greats by everyone in the business, yours truly included.

Did I mention he specialized in *crime scene* photography?

"Ironic, isn't it?" A slick young detective in a black leather jacket makes restating the obvious an artform. "Now the poor son of a gun *is* a crime scene."

"Stunning insight, Detective." I raise my camera and snap a shot of a particularly gruesome concentration of remains: a bloody mass of lumpy tissue splattered on a nearby wall. "I can hardly wait to read that scholarly discourse on the human condition I'm sure you've been working on."

The detective looks my way with eyes narrowed and bushy black mustache drooping at the corners. He strikes me as an undercover racist, the kind who gives an African-American guy like me a general impression of distaste without openly slinging his bigotry in ways that might get him in actual trouble. "What did you say your name is, again?" he asks.

"Cartesian. Omar Cartesian. And you?"

"Buchinsky." He says it with half a snicker, leaving off the first name.

"Good to meet you," I say, though it really isn't.

Sensing the clock is ticking on my crime scene access, I snap another shot of Sylver's remains with my Nikon FA SLR. It might not be a top-of-the-line camera, but it gets the job done every time. "So can you tell me, Detective Buchinsky, how this man became the subject instead of the photographer?"

A gray-haired, overweight medical examiner answers my question. "Looks like the victim was torn apart from the inside out," he says, continuing to collect swabs of blood from the floor. "Like something clawed him to shreds. If it wasn't for the driver's license and press pass in his wallet, we wouldn't have enough pieces to I.D. him without forensics."

"Any idea what might have torn him apart like that?" I keep snapping photos, all too aware that a crooked old beat cop I know and hate is looking my way and whispering in Buchinsky's ear.

"Swallowed a bobcat, maybe?" The medical examiner sighs and shakes his head at the mess on the floor. "Or a school of piranha?"

"Jesus." I snap another shot, this one of a wide-open window. Peering out, I see we're on the backside of the building...and I make a mental note. That window must be open for a reason.

I'm about to ask about it when I realize my time on the scene has expired. Out of the corner of my eye, I see Buchinsky break away from the beat cop and move in my direction.

"Cartesian." He reaches for the sleeve of my black trench coat...

...but I'm already quickstepping out of there, tightly clutching my Nikon with its load of murder scene shots that would have been highly prized by Sylver if he were still alive to sell them.

Fleetfooted as I am, I manage to hightail it down two flights of stairs and make it out on the street with body and soul—and exposed film—intact. Ducking police and police tape alike, I duck into the assembled crowd of looky-loos, glancing over my shoulder to make sure none of the fuzz are on my heels.

Half a block later, I double back and work my way around to the rear of the building. Cop-free—and dark as night, with nary a streetlamp to light the way—the place is a wasteland, littered with trash, junk, and—I'm certain—all manner of unpleasant nocturnal vermin.

Kicking through the overgrown weeds, I nearly trip on the very thing I'm seeking. As soon as I saw that open window upstairs, I knew *something* must have been thrown out of it...and here it is.

Reaching down, I lift the object out of the vegetation…and instantly recognize it as Sylver's personal camera.

It's a vintage Speed Graphic, bulky as hell, with a side-mounted flash rig—the same model used for decades by the most famous crime-scene shooter of us all, the great Weegee of New York City. Sylver used the same gear to follow in Weegee's footsteps, giving the same classic look to his photos, enhanced with his own modern-day twists.

Now here it is, dumped in the weeds outside the building where Sylver was killed—miraculously undamaged from the fall out of that window. Most interesting of all, though, based on the weight of the gear, are the camera's contents.

I am 99% sure, even without cracking the back of the thing, that there is undeveloped film loaded inside. I can only imagine, at least until I get to the darkroom at the newspaper where I work, what terrible secrets that film might hold.

11:15 P.M.

Should I have handed over Sylver's camera to the police? Probably…but I feel an obligation that runs deeper than the urge to perform my civic duty. After all, Sylver was a credit to our profession—a seeker of truth like myself. If that had been *me* splattered all over that tenement apartment, I would've wanted someone *like* me to get to the bottom of things…someone who wouldn't allow the truth to be buried by individuals and institutions seeking to cover their own asses and maintain the status quo.

At least, that's what I tell myself as the black-and-white photo prints come into focus in the chemical baths in the darkroom of my employer, *The Pittsburgh Seeker-Sentinel*. I just want a peek before I turn them over to the authorities, because I care…and besides, there's a story to be had.

Whatever killed Sylver, it wasn't run-of-the-mill; my gut says so, loud and clear, and it's rarely wrong. After all these years of running up against extraordinary phenomena in the course of my job—something that happens a lot more often than you might think—I've learned not to ignore it.

When the photos develop, I see yet again just how right that gut of mine can be.

The first one pinned to the drying line is a blur of motion, impossible to decipher. It isn't until I look at the second shot that I realize how good I had it with the first. *This* one very clearly shows Sylver Seaver in mid-annihilation, screaming his lungs out as his body is ripped to shreds by jagged ebony claws churning from inside.

By shot number three, Sylver's innards have mostly settled—some blocking the lens, from the look of it—and whatever ripped him open crouches amid the gore, dripping and glistening. I glimpse a bulging, inhuman eye, jagged spines…and something that could be either a suppurating sore or a gruesome maw rimmed with ulcerated flesh and gleaming fangs.

It's the *next* photo that's the biggest surprise, though. This one shows another corner of the room, as if the shooter finally turned away from Sylver's horrible fate—and I see the answer to a burning question: *Who* took the photos as Sylver was eviscerated, his shredded flesh and blood sprayed all over that tenement room?

The answer is clear: *she* did, the pretty twentysomething in the mirror with long blonde hair, holding Sylver's own Speed Graphic camera in her slender-fingered hands.

"Oh my God." Daphne Vargas, city editor of the *Seeker-Sentinel,* gapes at one of Sylver's photos through a cloud of smoke from her long, skinny cigarette. "That's Jenny Freemason!"

I roll down the sleeves of my black turtleneck sweater and frown across the desk on which the photos are scattered. It's a scene we've played out many times before—me presenting evidence in the closest thing Queen Vargas has to a throne room. Usually, the images involve everyday tragedies, crimes, or corruption…but every now and then, I bring her shots like these, capturing the extraordinary phenomena I've been in the habit of encountering on the job. I bring them to her again and again, proof of the supernatural at work in our midst—and Vargas, again and again, sweeps them aside with her usual sardonic quips and cigarette smoke.

She doesn't react that way this time, though. Her slender brown face turns pale and her mouth tightens, deep crinkles forming in her ruby lips. "Jenny is…*was* Seaver's assistant. Her father is a friend of mine."

"You have friends?"

"I've known *her* since she was a baby." She can't take her eyes off the photo. "Now what's she gotten herself mixed up in here?"

Some kind of demonic possession, possibly, I think, though I keep it to myself. "I'm not sure yet," is what I say aloud, then I clear my throat, feeling a twinge of sympathy for Vargas. We've worked together for over a decade and have a kind of love-hate relationship. "Daphne, we need to find her."

"Correction. *You* need to hand over that camera and these photos to the *cops* and let them do their job."

She's only saying what she has to—she's no friend of the establishment—but it bugs me, and I smack her desk with the palm of my hand. "This is above their *pay grade*. They're not *equipped* to deal with something like *this*."

Vargas glares at me. "And I suppose *you* are?"

I lean back, straightening the gold crucifix pendant on its chain around my neck. I'm not a man of great faith, but when you cross paths with some of the things I've seen in the shadows of this city, charms and totems can mean the difference between life and death, sanity and madness. "As a matter of fact…"

Vargas snatches the phone receiver out of its cradle and starts dialing. "I'm calling the cops right now, Cartesian…"

"*Trust* me." I jam down the buttons in the cradle, ending the call. "I brought home Maxine Hamilton's son, didn't I? And I found Luca Rosas when no one else could."

Vargas glares, but I've made my point. Her expression softens slightly, though of course she can't just admit to my face that I'm in the right. "You can't withhold *evidence* from the *police,*" she snaps.

It's time for me to beg, at least a little. "Daphne, *please*. Help me *find* her."

The boss of all she surveys gives me a good, long stare. The "hate" part of our relationship equation seems to be more prominent than the "love" right now.

Finally, she blinks and sighs. Her dark eyes flicker with deep-down worry…and a trace of hope. "What makes you think she's even still alive, Omar?"

A hunch? Wishful thinking? Experience with other freaks and their twisted hunting habits? "Just tell me,

Daphne. You know this girl. If she needed a safe place to hide, where would it be?"

Vargas turns and gazes out the window, thinking. I see my own reflection in the pane behind her, glasses glinting in the office's overhead lights, face framed by my close-cropped hair and beard.

I don't think she would ever admit it but we're allies in this fight, coming at the same challenge from different points of view…both knowing that in situations like this, we can best trust each other over almost anyone else alive.

"Sure, Cartesian." She turns, stubs out her cigarette in a beanbag ashtray, and reaches for a fresh one from the long, pink packet on the blotter of her desk. "I think I know just the place."

Monday, October 31, 1983, 12:30 A.M. – Halloween

Two guys in leather and fishnets stroll past me into the theater, singing a song about a transvestite.

"One, please." As I pay the old-timer at the ticket booth, he doesn't look twice at the big Speed Graphic camera hanging from my neck. For midnight showings of the particular cult movie now screening, bringing in oddball contraband is not only permitted, it's encouraged.

That's a good thing because I'm working on a theory and I'll need Sylver's camera to test it.

This isn't to say there's smooth sailing ahead, though. Even from the lobby, I can tell the show is: A, packed; and B, a good deal wilder than the matinee showing of *Splash*. It doesn't surprise me, since it *is* Halloween at this point; a high-energy horror show is to be expected.

When I crack open the auditorium door and slip inside, I see people in all manner of getups—most with an emphasis on leather, lace, and greasepaint—are dancing in the aisles. Many are ringing bells and heaving handfuls of uncooked rice at the screen, where a weird wedding is in progress.

None of them pays a lick of attention to the *Seeker-Sentinel* photographer in the black trench coat, turtleneck, and trousers with the old-school camera swinging from a tattered strap around his neck.

As *The Rocky Horror Picture Show* plays on the big screen, I take in the scene around me, looking for Jenny Freemason. According to Vargas, this is her favorite place to hole up, her go-to getaway spot when the going gets tough.

It's certainly a great place to hide out, especially during this particular showing. If that pretty young blonde is tucked away anywhere in this howling, costumed mob, the sideshow distractions are keeping her out of my sight.

At least at first. Just as I'm about to give up squinting at a particular row of seats in the back of the place, a group of revelers separate and I spot her. From what I can see, she's in immediate danger, and everyone else is having too much fun to notice.

Without hesitation, I spring into action.

As I push past the revelers and scramble up the narrow row, I see Jenny sprawled over the seats in a red sweater and jeans, thrashing and tossing her head as if she's undergoing a seizure. A leather-clad, face painted male of the musclebound variety is hovering over her in what appears to be a threatening manner…though it quickly becomes clear that there's more going on here than first meets the eye.

As I reach them, she grabs his face and hauls it down to her own. The guy looks surprised as she locks lips with him, planting the least romantic kiss I've ever seen (outside of my one and only mercy date with Vargas five years ago) on his bug-eyed visage.

No sooner does the kiss end than her body spasms and goes limp. As the guy wrenches away, I see a look of shock, as expected…but then, his expression suddenly twists into something different. Something *foul.*

He looks at me, and I freeze. Chills ripple up my spine, and I somehow *know.*

I was right about the demonic possession. The thing that got Sylver just jumped out of Jenny and into *him.*

I swing up Sylver's Speed Graphic and hastily aim the lens at the guy. I fire the shutter, the flash bursts to life, and I get the shot.

At which point, Mr. Musclebound leaps away, snarling, and charges past me like I'm not even there.

The auditorium door thuds shut behind him as I rush to the girl's side, expecting the worst. Instead, her eyes flicker open, and she gasps a lungful of air into a body that most certainly isn't dead.

When it comes to recovering from possession by a supernatural creature of unknown origin, can there be a better place than Darrell's All-Night Diner on Liberty Avenue? I think not. The fries and gravy alone are known far and wide as a balm to soothe the weary soul.

Not that anything other than hot black coffee will pass between Jenny's trembling lips just now. She's too upset, and rightly so, after what she's been through.

"Jenny?" I speak softly and cradle my own cup of joe, letting it warm my hands. "What can you tell me about what happened to you and Sylver?"

"Pure evil." Long blonde hair tangled and lusterless, face white as a sheet, she stares out the window at the neon-lit night life sliding past. "That's how it felt. Like being infected with *pure evil.* Taken over by something that wants to make you do the *worst things imaginable.*"

"I get the picture." I hike a thumb at the Speed Graphic beside me on the table. "Thanks to this."

"Sylver's camera." She nods. "It's special. It's the only way you can see that awful thing."

"Do you have any idea why? What makes this particular camera so unique?"

"It was one of *Weegee's* cameras," says Jenny.

I frown with disbelief. "The same *model* as Weegee's camera, you mean."

"I mean a camera that *belonged* to Weegee." She nods emphatically. "A camera Weegee actually *used.*"

"Wow." This is news to me. It hardly seems possible—but I go with it for now. "That's just *amazing.*"

"It really is," says Jenny. "Sylver paid a small fortune for it. The guy who sold it to him said it was magic, which was one of the secrets of Weegee's success...so Sylver bought it. And then he wished he hadn't. That *thing* started showing up in certain photos he took of murder scenes. It was like some kind of angel of death, present near corpses. Sylver didn't realize it actually went after the *living* and *caused* the fatalities...until it finally went after *him.*"

I know how the story ends, I can probably guess the rest...but I still need to hear it from her. "When Sylver died, were the two of you trying to stop this...angel of death?"

She nods sadly. "It was attached to an old man in the background of several murder scene photos. We tracked him down and tried to trap the angel with a special crystal Sylver bought, engraved with mystic runes and infused with holy water...but the thing jumped into Sylver instead." She wipes away a tear. "I tried driving it out of him with some incantations we'd found in an old grimoire, and you saw what happened. It literally tore Sylver apart and jumped into *me*."

I swallow a sip of coffee. "And now it's moved on." I don't like where this story is headed, with a deadly and malevolent body-swapping entity aggressively at large in a major metropolitan area...and me with no idea how to stop it. "The guy at the theater tonight, the one you kissed. Who was he?"

"Kissed?" She looks at me like I'm crazy. "What guy?"

"Skip dessert." I glance at the Speed Graphic with the exposed film tucked away inside. Though I don't yet have a plan for dealing with the creature, perhaps I might yet find some inspiration in Sylver's—and Weegee's—unique gear. "The proof of the pudding awaits us."

3:00 A.M.

Back in the *Seeker-Sentinel* darkroom, Daphne Vargas babysits Jenny while I develop the film from the Speed Graphic.

Vargas pats Jenny's shoulder sympathetically. "So how's that old man of yours doing, hon?"

"He still talks about you." Jenny looks and sounds steadier. Good for her, after everything she's been through. "You should give him a call."

"I will." Is that a catch I hear in Vargas's voice? I wonder if there might be more than mere friendship between her and Jenny's father. "You tell him I'll do that real soon."

"*Voilà!*" Just then, the print I've been working on comes into crystal clear focus in the tray of developer fluid.

Jenny moves closer for a look. "That's *it*." She shivers as she stares at the image. "That's the thing that killed Sylver."

There are some sights that human eyes aren't meant to see, and this, I'm fairly sure, is one of them. It's the clearest shot yet of the creature, complete with bulging eyes and a ragged maw lined with dripping fangs...but I'm more interested in the leather-clad, musclebound guy from the theater around whose throat and shoulders its claws are clamped. "So who is *he*?" I point a finger at the guy's face.

"A Starving Cannibal," says Jenny.

I move the print to the tray of stop bath, then the tray of fixer. "You're saying the creature drives the host to devour human flesh?"

Jenny shakes her head. "I mean he's Eddie Wilkins, the lead singer in a band *called* the Starving Cannibals. They're pretty popular on the local music scene these days."

"*How* popular?" I ask.

"They're playing a sold-out Halloween show tonight, actually," says Jenny.

There it is. That *sinking* feeling.

Serial demonic possessor plus sold-out concert (on Halloween night, no less) equals...

Nightmare.

An idea has been forming in my head, though, slowly taking shape as the print developed in its chemical baths. It might just give us a fighting chance against that thing.

Hanging the print on the line, I rush out of the darkroom and head straight for my desk with Vargas and Jenny close behind. Yanking open the bottom left drawer, I grab something I once received as a gag gift, something that I—serious news photographer that I am— never thought I'd have cause to use in the field.

"What on Earth are you up to now, Cartesian?" snaps Vargas.

"Haven't you ever seen an instant camera before?" I point the instant camera, push a button, and the flash fires...after which, a photo of Vargas's scowling kisser slides out of the front slot. I hand it to her with a flourish. "With a little ingenuity—and luck—it may yet prove to be our salvation."

"Whatever you say, Big Words." Vargas scowls and hikes a thumb in my direction for Jenny's benefit. "He can remind me he has a college degree all he wants, I still won't give him a raise."

"It's a master's degree, actually," I tell her with a grin. "And no, I *don't* expect a raise for reminding you about it...but I *do* expect one for saving the *city*."

Grabbing the Speed Graphic from my desk, I charge out of there with Jenny in tow, leaving Vargas shaking her head behind us.

4:30 A.M.

It has been my experience that the truest geniuses in the world live lives of cluttered desperation right under the noses of those who could most benefit from their miraculous works.

Exhibit A is an especially messy workshop in the dank and dismal basement of a disreputable optometry office in a rundown part of town. If you didn't know any better, you might not imagine said location as the home of a chronically insomniac genius tinkerer and the source of a potentially lifesaving apparatus...unless you're me, of course.

Would I buy glasses from the quacks upstairs? Never. Would I place my very survival in the hands of one Benjamin Franklin, 70-year-old self-taught expert in all things bright and shiny (not to be confused with the American inventor/diplomat/polymath of the same name)?

I wouldn't be standing in his workshop with Jenny Freemason, inhaling the copious secondhand smoke from whatever unidentifiable substance is burning in his Sherlock Holmes-style pipe if I didn't.

"What we're doing here." Franklin squints through the eyepiece of a jeweler's loupe at the lens he's just removed from Sylver's enchanted Speed Graphic. "I can't help feeling it's a desecration. This camera is *legendary*, is it not?"

"Sure." I wave away his concern and a particularly dense cloud of smoke at the same time. "But it's a matter of life and death."

Franklin's dark brown face crinkles as he fiddles with the loupe. "Nevertheless, a disclaimer is in order. Once I do as you've requested, this lens will no longer be usable as part of the Speed Graphic in your possession." He gestures at Sylver's camera on his cluttered workbench.

"We understand." I glance over at Jenny, who doesn't look so convinced...but she shrugs it off anyway. More than anyone in the room, she understands what's at stake if the angel of death is permitted to continue its rampage. She knows what it's like to have that awful thing occupying your body, forcing you to do its terrible bidding.

"If Sylver was a king among photographers, as many have claimed, then you, Mr. Cartesian, are asking me to ruin his Excalibur." Franklin lowers the loupe and meets my gaze, dead serious. "Can you live with that, Brother C?"

"I wouldn't be here otherwise."

"And Sylver's assistant, his Lady Lancelot?" Franklin puffs on the pipe as he turns to Jenny. "No qualms about sacrificing your mentor's legacy?"

"Will it work?" she asks.

"From a technical standpoint, I assure you this is a relatively simple matter. Time-consuming yet simple. Will it do what you *expect* it to, though? Might as well seek the answer to that one in a crystal ball." Franklin chuckles softly, then coughs.

"Can you have it ready by tonight?" I ask. "In time for the concert?"

He holds up the lens in one hand and the instant camera in the other. "That much, I can guarantee, Brother C. Desecration, I have found, takes nowhere near as much time as sanctification."

"You're a prince, Mr. Franklin." The more smoke I wave away, the more there seems to be. "And once your handiwork is done, we'll finally be able to *hunt* that thing. We'll be able to *see* it without developing film in a darkroom."

"*Not* that I'm guaranteeing it," adds Franklin. "Too many *x-factors* in the equation."

"Let's assume it *does* work as advertised." I spread my arms...then swing them inward, clapping my hands together. "Once we can quickly *see* the angel of death, we still need to figure out how to *catch* it...how to *trap* it."

"I have an idea about that." Jenny touches the body of the Speed Graphic on Franklin's workbench. "Though it means we'll have to take apart even more of Weegee's camera."

"The lens is already off." Franklin shrugs. "In for a penny, in for a pound, I suppose."

Arms folded over my chest, I reach up to rub my bearded chin. "Tell us more, Jenny. What's your idea for trapping that thing?"

"You definitely have *my* curiosity piqued," says Franklin. "What do you have in mind, pray tell?"

"How about if I show you?" She picks up one of Franklin's tools and uses it to pry off the back of the Speed Graphic's body. "Let's see if we can get lightning to strike more than once, shall we, Ben?"

Halloween Night, 7:30 P.M.

Hours later, Jenny and I—carrying Franklin's latest inventions unobtrusively on our persons—stand face to face with a burly security guard at the stage door of the theater where the Starving Cannibals are about to perform their big Halloween show. This particular guard, unfortunately, is taking his job seriously and making it his mission to keep us out of the backstage area.

"I understand where you're coming from," I tell him. "But how would it look if you turned away the very news team that could propel the Starving Cannibals to the pinnacle of international success and beyond?"

The beefy guard, packed into a black t-shirt and jeans, scratches his bushy, dark beard and narrows his eyes at us. "What's *beyond* international success?"

"Immortality!" I land a hand on his shoulder and lean in like a conspirator. "Such is the power of the free press in this great land of opportunity!"

"I'm sorry, but absolutely not." The guard folds his arms over his chest and shakes his pasty head. "A press pass isn't enough to go backstage at *this* show."

I'm just about to launch into a fresh tirade when I notice his right hand slowly rolling into a palm-up position, the universal symbol for the expectation of payment. The guard isn't so intractable, after all.

"Jenny?" I reach for my wallet and slide out two twenties. "Please remind me to invoice Aunt Daphne for this expense, won't you?"

"Will do." Jenny looks jumpy as she adjusts her cross-body messenger bag, the one loaded with two of Franklin's toys.

I plant the twenties in the guard's hand, but it takes another to open a gap to the doorway. I only hope it's worth it as we squeeze past Mr. Tough Guy into the glamorous world of show business, complete with a mangy rat—an actual rodent—scurrying across our path.

As we wander onward, the roar of the theater's sold-out crowd fills the hallway in excited anticipation. It only gets louder as we take a wrong turn that leads us onto the actual stage behind the closed curtain. Shooed away by a black-clad roadie, we quickly double back, taking a different turn this time.

Once we've found the correct hallway, the band's dressing room isn't hard to find at all. It's the one with "Starved for Cannabis" scrawled in magic marker over the band's actual name on a sheet of paper taped to the door.

I reach for the doorknob and pause, locking eyes with Jenny. "You okay?"

She nods, holding onto her bag with both hands. Everything we need is in there, except for what's hanging from a strap around my neck—another of the products of Ben Franklin's brilliant labors. I smile and tap it with the tip of a finger—the instant camera, modified and ready, its purpose in life about to be fulfilled.

"This one's for Sylver." That's what I tell her.

"For Sylver," she says with a quick nod.

"We can do this," I say. "We are *so* ready to finish this."

"I know." I see a flicker of fear in her eyes as she sets her jaw, preparing to confront the very thing that killed her mentor and made her life a living hell. (I still don't know everything she did while under its influence, and I'm a little afraid to find out.)

"We're going to beat this thing, I promise." I make sure there isn't any flicker of hesitation in my own expression, no hint of the actual apprehension I feel going into this confrontation.

Then, I knock and open the door at the same time, and we're committed.

"Hey, guys." I walk in like I own the place. "Meet your opening act!"

The five black-leather-clad musicians in the dressing room shoot us dagger eyes like they're going out of style. Given the general level of bad vibes in the place, if I had to guess which one of them harbors a rage-infused demonic passenger, I honestly couldn't say.

Between the two of us, Jenny and I will try to narrow it down some.

"Eddie!" Jenny grins and waves as if she isn't nervous at all. "Long time no see!"

The guy from the movie theater last night, the one who got a side order of supernatural possession with his big, sloppy kiss, points at the door. "You two can't be in here right now. We're about to go on stage."

"Which is *precisely* why we're here." I swing up the instant camera and snap a shot of him before he can duck or otherwise interfere. "To document the historic occasion of what will *surely* be the biggest breakthrough of your musical careers."

"Hey!" Eddie blinks away the flash. "What the hell?"

A print slides out of the camera's front slot, and I grab it. "Surely you've heard of *Rolling Stones* magazine, gentlemen?" The mistake in the way I say the title is intentional, meant as a diversion to give the photo time to develop.

As I flap the drying print, the band members crack up, Eddie laughing louder than any of them. "No such magazine, pal," he says. "Too plural."

I stop flapping and watch the image coalesce on the glossy paper. Since Franklin installed Sylver's modified lens on the instant camera, I should get revelatory prints much faster than I ever could with his antique Speed Graphic. I no longer have to run to a darkroom to see which musician is possessed by the angel of death...assuming it works. "Did I say *Rolling Stones*? What I meant to say was *Tiger Be—*"

I stop, surprised and disappointed at what I see on the paper...or, rather, *don't* see. Either the instant camera with the magic Weegee lens isn't working as expected...

...or Eddie does *not* have a supernatural possessor hiding under the hood.

"Say cheese, guys!" Without further ado, I whip up the camera and snap a shot of two of Eddie's buddies, then shoot the other two after that. Immediately, two prints feed out of the slot, one after another, and I grab them.

"Are you done?" Eddie looks *really* ticked now. "Can we finally go play our show for the *paying customers?*"

As the latest two photos develop, a wave of confusion washes over me. There isn't a single image of the angel of death in either of them.

"I don't understand." I hold up the photos for Jenny to see. "According to these, they're *all clear.*"

"Maybe it *moved on.*" Her eyes are wide, her voice tight. "Maybe it's already escaped into the *audience.*"

"Are you people *high?*" asks Eddie. "What are you even *talking* about?"

Just then, the door swings open, and a tall, silver-haired guy in a green plaid leisure suit and wide purple tie storms into the room. "You're *late*, Cannibals! If you don't get out there *now*, we'll have a *riot* on our hands."

"We're *trying*, Lou," says Eddie. "These two *nutjobs...*"

"No excuses!" snaps Lou. "Just get out there! I might be your *manager*, but there's *no way* I'm getting between you and a crazed mob of pissed-off fans!"

Without thinking, I whip the camera around and shoot Lou dead-on. The way he staggers back and hisses like Dracula with a faceful of holy water, I know we've finally found the subject of tonight's little drama.

Lou doesn't seem to appreciate the brightness of the flash, the special properties of Sylver's lens, or perhaps a combination of the two. He crashes against the wall, then shakes it off and spins, eyes darting in my direction.

I stay on the offensive, firing the instant camera again and again, photos pouring from the slot. Lou tries to block the light of the flash with his arms, but I keep it coming...even as I shout over my shoulder to my sister-in-arms.

"Jenny, get ready!"

Lou snarls, extending his hands like demonic claws. Just as he lunges, I hit him with another flash and sidestep his charge, sending him reeling to the floor.

"Do it!" I shout. "Do it now!"

Jenny has the mirrors out of her bag—each one a square panel, twenty inches on a side—and dashes over to hand one to me. Just as Lou lurches to his feet, we take up positions—me in front of him, her behind him.

At which point, the mirrors facing each other create an optical illusion. Lou—and the angel of death possessing him—sees endless reflections of himself, marching into infinity.

It's a common phenomenon, we've all seen it before...but this time, it's special. Thanks to Benjamin Franklin's technical wizardry, each panel is coated with a thin film of melted glass obtained from the internal mirrors pried from Sylver's magically-enhanced Speed Graphic camera. The result is quite a bit more impressive than any optical illusion.

Caught between the mirrors and driven by the thing that possesses him, Lou clutches his head and emits an unearthly howl. He sinks to his knees, and we follow, keeping him bracketed between the facing reflective surfaces.

"Nooooo!" Lou gasps and gags, and I worry. The biggest question mark in my plan is the possible sacrifice of an innocent host.

But Lou doesn't explode in gory splatters and chunks like Sylver did...and the angel of death doesn't give up its hold on him. Instead, the creature makes him knock the mirror from Jenny's hands, dashing it to pieces on the floor.

With one mirror gone, the connection breaks. No longer trapped by the infinite progression of images, Lou leaps to his feet and charges from the room, bowling me over *en route*. I see him hook a sharp left in the corridor, and the blood turns to ice in my veins.

I know where he's going, where he *has* to be going...and it's the worst possible outcome, the one Jenny and I came here to prevent.

"After him," I say as she helps me up. "We need to stop him *now.*"

"He's going *there*, isn't he?" she asks. "The auditorium."

"Yes." I tighten my grip on the last remaining mirror and head for the door in Lou's wake. "The perfect place for a body-hopping angel of death. He's heading straight for the *audience.*"

Once unleashed in a crowd, the angel of death acts at dizzying speed. Even as we run down the hallway, I hear the sounds of chaos up ahead, the sounds of people pitted against each other in full-tilt combat.

When Jenny and I run into the backstage area, the noise is louder than ever—a cacophony of shouts and screams and curses and cracks and impacts. Stepping out on the stage, we shade our eyes against the glare of the spotlight and see the auditorium filled with battling audience members, a multitude driven by a series of rapid-fire possessions to attack each other with no holds barred.

How long until someone gets killed, if they haven't already? How many of them are on the way to crippling injuries or mutilations? The possibilities are terrifying.

This is the very nightmare I'd hoped to prevent. Now, somehow, we have to figure out a way to stop it before it gets any worse.

"What do we do?" As Jenny asks the question, one of the theater seats flies up from the crowd and crashes across the stage, barely missing us.

My mind races. Somewhere in that sea of struggling humanity, the angel of death is hard at work—but how can we find it, let alone stop it? The thing is moving too fast from body to body for the instant camera to effectively identify a target host…and even if it could, the information wouldn't do us any good. Except for one mirror, we are weaponless, and that remaining mirror is utterly useless on its own.

Or is it?

The outlines of a plan start to form as I squint at the source of the spotlight, blazing from an elevated platform around a booth on the far wall of the auditorium. I turn my gaze upward then, scanning the lighting grid hung from the vaulted ceiling. I see lights of all sizes aiming in various directions, most dark. I see speakers, as well, also angled in different directions…and something else, suspended from the middle of the grid, slowly turning.

Turning and glittering.

"Come on!" I bolt back the way we came, heading for the hallway. We need to take the long way around to our destination; battling through the brawl on the floor of the auditorium is *not* an option.

"Where are we going?" asks Jenny, breaking into a run to keep up.

"The control booth," I tell her. "I have an idea."

"What kind of idea?"

"A *long shot*," I shout over my shoulder. "I'm thinking *disco* might not be so dead *after* all."

The control booth, when we reach it, is wide open and deserted—a lucky break for us.

"What exactly are we doing here?" Jenny has to yell to make herself heard over the chaos in the auditorium.

It gets even louder when I open the door leading out to the platform around the booth. Stepping through the doorway, I wave for her to follow.

The platform's metal grate flooring supports the big spotlight projector, which is currently still aimed at the stage. Steering it with one hand while holding on to the remaining magic mirror with the other, I swing the beam up and along the grid, searching for the object I spotted earlier from below.

I find it fast, its faceted surface catching the spotlight's beam: a mirror ball, left over from the disco craze of the 1970s. Someone must have switched it on for the Starving Cannibals show, because it's turning slowly, throwing flashes of reflected light in all directions— including over the battling mob in the auditorium.

"Here." I hand the mirror panel to Jenny. "Use this to direct the beam at the disco ball. Make sure the light bounces off this plate first."

Jenny's eyes widen with understanding. "Give it the magic touch first, huh? Will do!" Jaws clenched, she hurries to the front of the projector with the mirror panel in hand, complete with its special coating of melted glass from Sylver's enchanted Speed Graphic.

Holding tight to the mirror so as not to drop it into the brawling mob, Jenny leans out over the metal railing and tips the panel at an angle into the projector's beam. Deflected, the bright white beam shunts from the center of the disco ball, instead catching a nearby span of the gridwork from which the ball is suspended.

"Adjusting!" I shout over the pandemonium from below, which seems to be escalating by the minute. "Moving it left a few inches!"

Jenny leans back with the mirror in hand, waiting. Holding on to the grips, I shift the nose of the projector to the left as promised, trying to compensate for the altered angle of the beam when the panel interrupts its linear flow.

"Now try it!" I yell.

This time, when Jenny tips in the magic panel, it angles the beam to strike the right hemisphere of the disco ball. *Almost there.* "One more tweak!" I tell her.

Jenny leans away again, and I nudge the projector slightly left. When she tips in the plate again, the angle is finally perfect. The spotlight hits the ball dead center, flaring off the many tiny mirrors on its surface and showering the audience below with swirling sparks.

This is it, the last-ditch attempt—the only idea I have for beating this thing. I can only hope that the beam from the spotlight, splintered and spread by the disco ball, will carry the same miraculous properties as any light that comes in contact with the lens or mirrors from Sylver's magic camera.

My hope looks to be unfounded, though. The only change I see in the audience is the blanket of disco ball sparks flowing over them. Otherwise, they keep pummeling, kicking, and clawing at each other with abandon, caught up in the scuffle inflicted by the body-swapping angel of death sweeping through them like a scirocco.

Panic sets in and, sweating from the heat of the spotlight, I instinctively reach for the knob controlling the brightness. I crank it hard to the right, all the way up, and pray the projector doesn't blow from the strain.

The beam pouring out through the aperture intensifies. Jenny shuts her eyes and turns her head away but never lets go of the mirror panel or changes its angle.

The intensified beam blasts the disco ball, and the reflected sparks flare brighter than ever on the battling crowd. This time, the effect is much different than before. The audience members don't ignore the light and continue their murderous strife.

Instead, they all collapse at once, dropping like puppets whose strings have been cut.

After they've fallen, a plume of black smoke—lit from within by crackling arcs of crimson lightning—curls from one of the inert bodies sprawled on the floor. It ripples and billows as it rises like some flower out of Hell, blossoming with dark, infernal power...then coalesces in midair, taking on the familiar form of the grotesque creature from the photos Sylver, Jenny and I shot.

The thing glares in our direction with its single bulging, bloodshot eye. I am mesmerized as its ulcerated maw twists open, exposing a ring of gleaming fangs and emitting a piercing shriek, a sound straight out of a nightmare. Then, suddenly, ragged wings unfold from its humped back, and it leaps toward us with its jagged, ebony claws extended.

"Zap it!" shouts Jenny. "Hurry!"

At that moment, we spring into action, moving in swift and perfect concert. As I swing the projector toward the beast, Jenny keeps the magic mirror angled in its blazing beam of light.

Before the creature can dive from its path, the spotlight meets it head-on, washing its awful form with a cascade of radiance. The thing howls and writhes frantically against the current—then explodes in a spray of darkling shards.

Only then do I finally switch off the spotlight.

"Oh my God." Jenny slumps against the railing. "We got it."

"We did." My heart's pounding so hard, I feel like I might be the next one to explode. "But it was one hell of a close call."

Jenny looks down at the motionless bodies strewn across the auditorium. "That thing was a lot more powerful than we knew. I swear, it was possessing *most* of those people at one time."

"Maybe it got stronger as it went along." I stand beside her, gazing down with stunned regret. "I just hope most of the victims lived through it."

Jenny shakes her head and sighs. "I really don't want to go down there."

"Me neither." I reach over and pat her shoulder. "Come on, we'll do it together."

Four Months Later
Wednesday, February 29, 1984, 8:05 P.M.

What kind of exhibit serves cheap rotgut liquor as a cocktail and filterless cigarettes as *hors d'oeuvres?*

The same kind of exhibit that's held in a dark, dismal basement in a back alley in a sketchy part of Pittsburgh…an exhibit of the not-so-famous work of the famous—and recently deceased—crime scene photographer, Sylvester Seaver (whose vices of choice were rotgut and filterless cigarettes, by the way).

In other words, exactly the kind of exhibit that someone like me would get an invitation to.

"Omar!" As soon as I walk through the door, Jenny Freemason—self-appointed defender of Sylver's legacy and curator of the exhibit—hurries over with two tumblers of amber liquid in hand. Even in this dank environment, she manages to look bright-eyed and perfectly put-together in a sparkling black dress and sky-high heels. "So glad you could make it!"

"Well, you *did* pique my curiosity." I hoped she might give me a hug, but I settle for the offered tumbler of rotgut instead. "Something in the invitation about a *surprise* I wouldn't want to miss out on?"

"Right this way."

As I follow her, I'm impressed by how together she seems—apparently completely recovered from her ordeal with the angel of death. In the months since I saw her last, in the wake of the angel's rampage at the Starving Cannibals show, she has clearly come a long way. Not only has she gotten back to work shooting crime scenes—starting with the aftermath of the angel-directed riot (which, mercifully, ended with zero fatalities)—but she has organized and opened this exhibit dedicated to her mentor.

She leads me through the exhibit now, where framed, blown-up versions of Sylver's murder scene photos—specifically, those that feature the angel of death—hang on black scrim panels.

I nod approvingly. "There are more than I expected."

"And more right over here." She leads me to another display, this one featuring a jumble of unenlarged photos from an instant camera...photos that are very familiar to me. "*This* is the surprise, Mr. Cartesian."

"Well, well." I can't help smiling. "You shouldn't have." The quality is poor, as is often the case with such photos, but the subjects are clear enough. Lou, the manager of the Starving Cannibals, is front and center in each one, with the hideous visage of the angel of death hovering over him, attached to his physical form by means of its glistening ebony claws.

"It's the least I could do," says Jenny. "And I'd like to make you an offer, if I may."

"Yes?"

"We want to keep this going," explains Jenny. "Make it a secret museum, dedicated to works that would not otherwise see the light of day. Works that capture things lurking beneath the surface of everyday life...images that might otherwise be suppressed by a fearful society intent on maintaining the status quo."

"Suppressed, you say?"

"I've followed your work, Omar. It occurs to me that one such as yourself might encounter such images in the course of his endeavors as a photojournalist...images that perhaps tell the *other* half of the stories that your publisher may be too timid to print in full."

"Interesting notion." She's right on target with the part about the timid publisher...and the rejected photos that tell the other half of the sanitized stories that appear in the *Seeker-Sentinel*.

As if on cue, I hear the laugh of *Seeker-Sentinel* City Editor Daphne Vargas and see the smoke from one of her skinny cigarettes drift up from behind a nearby scrim.

Of course she got an invite, given her friendship with Jenny's father—and her presence punctuates my thoughts of job dissatisfaction.

How many times have I submitted sensational photos of shocking phenomena to Vargas, only to have them buried? Too many to count. So many, it makes me want to give up the fight sometimes.

But then, I help someone like Jenny to overcome a supernatural threat and get her life back, and I realize there's more to it than recognition.

"So what do you say, Omar? Do you have anything other than these?" Jenny hikes a thumb at the instant photos. "Anything you might like to exhibit at the Sylver Seaver Secret Museum of the Macabre?"

I smile and raise my glass. The truth is, a little recognition isn't a bad thing every now and then…though coming off as too eager never did anyone any good, they say. "Your invitation is much appreciated, Ms. Freemason, though nothing springs to mind at the moment."

Jenny shrugs. "Perhaps you could look around a bit and see what you've got in your personal archives?"

"Oh sure. Who knows?" Grinning, I clink my tumbler against hers. "Maybe something will turn up."

Armageddon's Eve

Steve Oden

Several doors hiss closed behind them as the blind bear and his bodyguard follow directional lights deep inside the UFO's dark spinning structure. They are being led somewhere. So far, no one has greeted them, nor have they heard voices. The silence is unbroken, even by mechanical noises.

Adderlene, the scout snake, leads. The rebel supreme commander grasps her tail, feeling somewhat embarrassed when he imagines what the pair must look like: a four-meters long slithering serpent with her sensor and weapons hood spread, followed by a battered, scarred toy bear in a torn and mud-splattered uniform.

What an unimpressive way to introduce themselves to the operators of this amazing vehicle, he thinks.

"I don't know what came over me to insist that we walk through that hatch when it opened," he whispers to the snake. "Over your strenuous objections, of course." The bear's welfare is her responsibility, but how can a mere soldier overrule the leader of armies?

"Sss-ilence would be helpful right now, sssir." The snake stops, embarrassed by her words. A private giving advice to a grand general. The blind bear feels her tail-tip vibrate in consternation.

"Junction ahead. No more arrow light-sss. Request permission to reconnoiter," she says.

He knows Adderlene means to draw fire down on herself if they've encountered a trap. He can't allow such a sacrifice. It's time for him to start acting like the supreme commander, even if he doesn't look like one.

"No, I will go first. On behalf of the Free Toys and our allies, my job is to greet whoever has invited us on their vessel."

He walks forward, keeping both paws in contact with Adderlene's cylindrical body.

"By the way, do you feel a lightness? It almost seems that I could float away..."

A voice blares: YES, IT'S THE EFFECT OF OUR GRAVITRONIC CORE.

The snake coils around her leader protectively, unlimbering a grenade launcher with prosthetic limbs built into the weaponry hood. Lenses drop down over both eyes, giving her stereoscopic vision for aiming and infrared imaging.

She tastes the air with her forked tongue for the presence of toxic gas or the release of pheromones by nervous ambushers ready to attack. Whatever the threat, she will fight viciously and give up her life to keep the blind bear out of their clutches.

Overhead lights flash on, focusing on a ramp that leads upward to a platform where someone—or *something*—waits in the shadows. Adderlene can see the object with her vision enhancements and zeroes in the sighting reticule of the grenade launcher. It's a hunched figure, gray-robed and hooded. Shorter than the bear, or perhaps the forward-leaning posture is playing tricks. A long, fleshy tail balances the creature.

The supreme commander feels her go rigid. He doesn't realize the scout snake's reptile brain is reacting to a long-ago muscle memory passed down from her ancestors.

"What is it?" he asks.

She hesitates, never taking her eyes off the target, but hisses, "Isss a rat! A big rat…"

Toy Soldier looks around the table at his commanders and staff advisors. Despondent faces look back. They understand his decision to delay the attack until the blind bear can be rescued—wherever he is, whatever his condition.

"We have never lost a fight that he planned and executed," Toy Soldier says. "The battle plans for this last, all-out attack are in his head…not written down anywhere. We know the bits and pieces that affect our regiments and brigades: the positioning of assets, target goals, timing. But how does it all fit together and what might happen when we finally engage the enemy?"

He taps the side of his head with a finger. "It's all stored in his remarkable strategic and tactical brain."

Nods from the staffers and most of the brass. Not complete agreement, however.

Brigadier General "Mac" McCallen can't sit still. The Scottish terrier's front paws are on the table, claws skittering on the polished wood.

"But, Sirrah!" growls the bearded leader of the war dogs who captured and held the Bloody Bridge, giving rebel forces a major victory and positioning them to win the war. "Pardon this old dog's impertinence, but aren't ye keen enough in the supreme commander's wiles and ways to lead us?"

All eyes turn to the velveteen biological toy. That he has the courage to say what they are thinking dispels some of the depressive mood in the room.

"Ta delay attacking those poppy-cock bairns might be a curse on us all. That grand bear got us here, an' he meant to end it here," McCallan says.

"Whit's fur ye'll no go by ye!"

The proud dog barks and jumps on the table, standing to attention and preparing to receive his dressing down or demotion.

Toy Soldier stares and looks dumbfounded. "Explain that last phrase."

A white-bearded old man dressed in red and seated at the end of the table laughs. General Santos von Clausewitz is the mercenary leader formerly under contract to the children's kingdoms. He now leads the Legion of Free Elves, allied with the rebels.

"Commander, allow me to interpret." He smiles broadly and explains, "It's a Gaelic proverb. It means have faith in yourself...like all of us have confidence in your ability to conduct this battle and achieve the final victory."

"Aye!" yips McCallen. "Could'na said it better mah-self."

One by one, the Free Toy and allied military leaders stand, salute, and give reports on their readiness. Each one concludes by pledging to follow Toy Soldier to glory or hell.

Captain Sea Foam is the last.

"Sir, we are ready to insert the Dollies. A decision to proceed with the attack needs to be made."

Toy Soldier remembers the words of his mentor. A leader is someone who makes the difficult decisions, doesn't shirk his one-and-only duty: winning, despite the costs, if it will bring peace and wipe out evil.

Decision made, he executes a slow, meaningful return salute and holds it as his eyes fix each subaltern in turn.

"Set the attack clock and get your units in jump-off positions. I will send out revised plans, if necessary. You know what's at stake. Push and keep pushing. Let me worry about the rest."

The hurrahs went on for several minutes, led by the howling of the Scottish terrier toy still standing atop the table.

An infantry company of human girls from the newly allied Banfeinni Brigade—fierce, teenaged, female warriors in the ancient Irish tradition—silently advances, mounted in light armored vehicles equipped with the latest stealth shielding and background projectors.

Their mission is a reconnaissance in force preceding kickoff of Operation Extinguish in two days. Their vehicles thread hills of rubble and bomb craters. The objective is a row of warehouse-sized structures recently ceded by the enemy.

One of the pock-marked buildings is huge. Six stories high, with poured gel-steel walls five feet thick, designed to absorb high-velocity cannon fire and missile hits, it looms ominously in the roiling dust. Kingdom forces fighting a rear action to cover the main army's retreat didn't easily give up this piece of ground.

Captain Alva, named for a daughter of Celtic King Cormac mac Art, wipes grime from her freckled cheeks and wonders why. She turns to her favorite fleet-footed scout-runner and says, "I think 'tis curious there'd be savage firefights over yonder ugly lump. I want a patrol to get inside, put eyeballs on what caused our foes to fight so stubbornly to keep it!"

"Aye, Cap'n!" Corporal Maeve, dressed in a fade-out suit of druid-tech design, salutes before dismounting through the rear hatch of the command vehicle. Neither her nor her captain are yet 18 years old, but they distrust modern battlefield communications whenever the balloon might go up and put lives on the line. Old ways, the ones their ancestors used, are more reliable.

She is proud that Captain Alva left it up to her to choose the team. The brigade is famed for its recon capabilities, but this company ranks at the top of the heap—and Sergeant Orla's team is the best-of-the-best.

The runner appears as nothing more than a cloud shadow in the ruins as she rounds up the patrol and scouts ahead for ingress and retreat routes through the bones of a formerly thriving civilization: twisted girders, melted glass, and waste pits where once sky-stabbing towers reflected light from mirrored sides…all the glory of achievement fades in the hate and murderous rage of war.

But it's a good place to hide, burrowing like beetles in the dirt to make observations and gather intelligence.

Maeve finds a yawning underground entrance unblocked by debris. It opens on a vast assembly floor over which arch four thick pillars built of coiled tungsten ultra-steel. These are the corner supports for what appears to be an outlandish industrial cathedral. Various large gears, spokes, pulleys and chains depend from platforms high above.

The expanse is so large, it appears almost empty. But Maeve notes it has been used recently. Greasy tire tracks, piles of garbage, abandoned ammunition crates, stacks of small arms, caches of canned food, and a row of electric generators are evidence of the building's interrupted occupancy.

There are also mysterious lab equipment, banks of computers, and a half dozen armored drone crawlers with anti-personnel missiles still in the launching pods.

The scout thinks, *Hmmm . . . the defenders left all this behind. Expensive and valuable stuff. They were in a hurry."* She decides to inventory the remaining contents of the interior by releasing a swarm of tiny camera bots.

From basement floor to roof, the vertical core of the building is expansive. Large industrial cranes and mobile platforms sit idle in the shadows. Cables and chains capable of mooring a battleship crisscross what appears to be a space devoted to assembly and testing.

Maeve scratches under her helmet, where reddish bristles of once silken hair itch. One of the bots has transmitted an image that disturbs and amazes at the same time.

The patrol catches up. Sgt. Orla nods and whispers, "Good work, dearie. Let me take the gals and see why them kingdom slinkers defended this cold, drafty damned cave for so long."

"I might already know," Maeve says, starting to climb a ladder to an overhead platform. Orla is right behind her. She is slightly older than most of the Banfeinni warriors, more experienced in warfare and hard to rattle.

Looking down, the sergeant gasps. "Mother Mary and all the saints! What did that?"

Four deep furrows have been gouged in the thick steel floor of a giant hydraulic platform. The metal curls outward, like shavings from a lathe. Corpses of a dozen liveried kingdom soldiers lie squashed or dismembered on the adjacent ground, along with mangled lab-coated individuals who Maeve suspects were engaged in weaponry development and manufacture.

"They were hiding something here," she tells Orla. "Something gigantic and deadly."

Pointing to the furrows, she says, "Those are claw marks! We must report back to headquarters. They have a secret weapon—a monster of some type—like nothing we ever imagined."

Before the sergeant can issue a platoon recall, one of the Banfeinni privates arrives with a dire warning.

"Beg to report," she says, out of breath from climbing down from another high platform. "This building is mined! We found a powerful explosive device on a timer up there." She points upward to the shadows. "The roof will come down on our heads at any moment."

Although Orla doesn't want to break radio silence, the others must be alerted. She tongue-clicks a retreat signal into the microphone sewn on her uniform collar, then yells at those nearby in Gaelic.

"*Rith le d'anam!*"

Run for your lives...

Princess crouches with the rearguard squad of Dollies in the lee of a shell-damaged bunker. They are deep in the defensive arc protecting Count Thaddeus's remaining territory. Half a klick to the rear is the muddy, debris-filled river where Sea Foam monitors enemy activity with a sensor array raised from the submergible that landed them.

So far, the enemy remains deaf and blind. Their patrols seem listless, perhaps lulled by lack of activity shown by the rebels. Perfect for the Dollies, who are slipping out of wetsuits and donning their costumes and porcelain masks.

They have counterfeit passes allowing passage through enemy lines as a group of dancers. They're scheduled to entertain at a gathering of kingdom leaders hosted by the count.

The Princess admires the brazenness of Dolly Bright Eyes and her sisters. Hiding in plain sight, they will draw every kingdom soldier's eye, swirling and pirouetting down the narrow streets in gossamer dresses of rainbow colors.

It works perfectly. The troupe passes unhindered through checkpoints. Teen sentinels barely glance at their fake papers. Instead, they are mesmerized by the mysterious and exotic masked performers.

Under those masks, Princess realizes, is not beauty, but scars very similar to her own. The Dollies are girls who suffered horrible disfigurement at the hands of a twisted kingdom leader: the late and unlamented Turko Shem.

Kept in a harem until their time came to please the human monster, each dancer comes away mutilated, branded forever by the youth ruler's cruelty and instruments of torture. Until Dolly Bright Eyes. Using Shem's own knife to gut him, she escapes after rounding up her sisters and others. They find haven with the rebels, where a blind bear sends them to train at a monastery, specializing in oriental close-quarters fighting techniques and stealth. The Dollies become a troupe of entertainers with deadly prowess.

Most think the masks hide their identities, but Princess knows better. She has a hard time resisting a feeling of sisterhood with her fellow Dollies, but can't allow such soft-hearted emotion to get in the way of her revenge. Until the opportunity presents itself to kill Toy Soldier and the bear, she will be part of this sisterhood of assassins.

They pass through rings of defense—mined roadways, interlocking fields of fire for heavy-caliber automatic weapons, ranged killing ground for fire-and-plunge mortar shells and anti-tank blockades rigged with high explosives—on their way to the enemy's hidden headquarters in the rubble of the Count's once majestic castle.

Led to the secret entrance of the command bunker, leering soldiers check them for hidden weapons or signal-broadcasting devices on which smart bombs could home. They are approved for entry and allowed to keep their fans, extra clothing, cosmetics, and combs.

Suddenly, a blinding light flares toward the river; a thunderous roar and rain of debris from the sky follows. The landscape of shell-razed buildings, standing like old tombstones in a forgotten cemetery, is swallowed in a rolling dust cloud.

The Dollies are quickly herded into the bunker, where the Count's major-domo greets them. A wide, greasy smile paints his pimpled face.

"Ah, my ladies. Welcome. Tomorrow night, you will perform for mighty kingdom leaders who represent the united front that will put down the rebel alliance once and for all," he boasts.

Dolly Bright Eyes replies, "The honor is all ours, but are we safe here?"

"In case you're wondering about the distant explosion and artillery fire, I am pleased to announce that a major incursion by the so-called freedom fighters has failed. They walked into a trap, and none survived. It was a slaughter!"

"You put our minds at rest, thank you."

"Just in case you have further trepidation about this complex and its security, let me give you a guided tour on the way to your quarters," offers the major-domo with a lascivious stare at the Dolly leader.

"Oh, please do. We're only timid dancers, of course...not brave warriors."

Her bright eyes sparkled hypnotically, and soon he is under her control. Yes, they'd learn everything about the bunker and the kingdom leaders expected to attend the meeting. And the major-domo will never remember he told them about the number of guards and staff, secret passages, emergency exits, armories, communications center, private suites, and barracks.

Maeve, covered by rubble, waits in the bottom of the hole she found.

The scout is not alone. Squad-mates occupy the deep, oddly shaped depression. Like her, they wait for secondary explosions before digging out. Her shelter-and-rally signal a few seconds before the structure came down might have saved a score of Banfeinni troopers.

The scout wiggles toes and fingers, flexes her elbows and knees, feels for broken bones or wounds. She finds nothing severe, except for minor cuts and bruises. Maeve stands and coughs concrete dust raining from the massive cloud overhead.

Sgt. Orla is already counting heads and evaluating the injured. She nods at the scout.

"Good work, again! If ye hadn't found this pit, our arses would ha' been blowed to bloody flinders."

"Just luck, this time. I fell into the damned thing. Not a bit of heroism was involved," Maeve explains.

Incoming fire now adds insult to injury. The enemy starts to pour in antipersonnel shells, firing blind but raking the blast site.

"Time to go, dearies!" shouts the sergeant. "Powder yer noses and don't fergit to keep low. Wait for ma signal."

"Do you notice anything about this hole?" Maeve asks, pointing to the thick layer of punctured steel, beneath which is a meter of fiber-reinforced concrete and another meter of quarried stone. "This was done by something very heavy."

The hole is also an odd shape, the edges clean—not ragged like a shell crater—with four furrows like trenches extending beyond the cavity.

"Well, as holes in the ground go, I ain't the expert. What're ye blatherin' about?" Orla says, preparing for a fighting retreat.

"Tis not a hole at all," the scout marvels.

She gestures at the deep depression that has saved most of the squad. "It's a footprint."

WELCOME TO OUR INTERPLANETARY VESSEL…YOU ARE IN NO DANGER.

The words blast from hidden speakers in the walls.

YOU ARE HONORED GUESTS AND WILL BE TREATED AS EMMISARIES.

The robed rat begins to shuffle down the ramp.

"Sss-ir?" the scout snake asks, tracking the approaching figure with her weapon.

"Stand down, Adderlene," the Blind Bear commands. "This may be our chance to unravel the mystery of the UFOs and why they are here."

The rat pulls back its hood, exposing a gray and grizzled head with a twitching pink, pointed nose.

"My name is Burl Sook, ambassador for the Solaris Commission," the rat says.

He takes the bear's paw in his. "And you are the famed leader of the rebel alliance. We have watched from afar your struggles against the kingdom tyrants. Believe me, we know full well how innocents are victimized, even murdered by unfeeling monsters in human form!"

The handshake is firm, and the rat bows. "This is why we are here," he says.

The bear hears no malice or cunning in the rat's voice. He asks, "What is your purpose?"

Burl Sook straightens as much as he can. His back is painfully bent, it appears. Whether by age or injury is hard to tell. But he smiles warmly and answers.

"We have journeyed to your war-torn planet to broker a peace treaty, of course."

The Thing in The Subway
Steven Van Patten

The cop's eyes squinted.

Kyle wondered if the officer was trying to look intimidating or if he was just nearsighted. "What do you want me to say?" He shrugged as the cop stepped closer, his narrowed eyes filled with menace.

"Just tell me what you saw." The cop seemed irritated.

Kyle's eyes found the badge glistening on the officer's chest. Franklin. 5368.

"This guy jumped the turnstile. He did-didn't have a shirt on." Kyle managed to say.

"Did he do something out of the ordinary?"

Kyle shook his head. He couldn't believe he was going through this. "Fuck yeah! He jumped into the tracks." Reliving the whole thing, seeing it in his head again, made him shake involuntarily.

"And then what?"

"He was shouting something, but I couldn't make it out. I had my headphones on and its echoey in here."

"What happened next?"

"Then the guy crawled over this nearby track and to the third rail and he laid across it."

The officer's face brightened suddenly, as though Kyle's questioning was finally getting somewhere. "And he wasn't electrocuted?"

"Didn't seem like it. But I never know what that's about. I've seen track workers step on that thing and nothi—"

"Did you see what happened next?"

"Yeah, well he was laid across and then he stuck his head out into the express track just as that train came through."

"How fast would you say that train was going?"

Kyle took an involuntary step back. *What the fuck is wrong with this cop? Why does he seem almost happy about this shit?* "The top speed, I guess. Thirty, forty miles an hour maybe?"

"And?"

"Well, I turned away after that?"

"You turned away?" The officer's tone seemed to imply that Kyle was less than manly for averting his gaze as a man killed himself in the subway tracks.

"Yes!" He shook his head. "I turned away and started calling 9-1-1. Only while I was waiting for the call to connect, I turned to see the man and he was upright and climbing back onto the platform?"

"He wasn't hurt?"

Kyle shook his head again. "No. No blood. No nothing. He was just there. Climbing back up and headed towards me."

"So, you got a good look at him?"

"Yes."

Over the cop's shoulder, Kyle could see the train pulling in. The seven people who had also been on the platform when the shirtless man appeared, readied themselves to get onboard. A teenaged girl, probably

Dominican, with a purple streak running through what would otherwise be raven-black hair was the only one who had bothered to turn and look back at him with any concern. The rest took their anticipatory steps forward as they waited for the train to stop.

The officer seemed oblivious to his other potential witnesses leaving the scene, or that Kyle would now be late to wherever he was going. "Tell me what he looked like."

"Well, he was a white guy. Dirty, like he'd fallen out of a chimney or some shit. He was also barefoot. Red-brownish hair."

The officer smiled, as if he'd been accidentally cheered up. "And he confronted you?"

"He ran up to me and grabbed me by my shirt. He shouted something about not being able to die."

"An odd thing to say," the officer observed.

"I guess." Kyle was confused. Did the cop want his opinion? That certainly would have been a first.

"Which way did he go?"

"Down into the tunnel." Kyle pointed in the direction the train was leaving. "That way."

As the train rumbled out of the station, the cop stood quietly watching. For a moment, he and Kyle were bathed in a series of shadows and flashes. Then it all went still.

Without so much as a 'thank you' the cop walked away from Kyle, seemingly headed down in the tunnel to find the shirtless man.

Kyle turned to look at the LED ARRIVALS sign. The next train wasn't for ten minutes.

"Motherfucker," he said under his breath. Anger welled up in his chest. He would be late for the job interview he was headed to. His mind scrambled as he contemplated his options. He could try to run out and get an Uber, but traffic and the price-gouging that normally happens in the morning would leave him broke and late, instead of just late. He could report the officer, but seriously, what would that accomplish?

You could have just told the cop you had a job interview.

"He probably would have arrested me, just to make sure I didn't get the job." He said out loud. He knew it was a ridiculous thought, but if one thing the internet had taught him over the years is that ridiculous things happen to black people all the time. Ridiculous and harmful.

He glanced back at the ARRIVALS sign. Nine minutes. *Ugh!*

He actually felt the scream before he heard it. A guttural bellow sounding from the tunnel where the cop had left the platform. His insides trembled as his mind ran amok. *Where is this asshole's back up? Is it the cop killing the guy or the guy killing the cop? He just cost me a job, now I have to get him rescued.*

He turned and walked briskly towards the turnstiles. The booth clerk (can't call them token clerks anymore, they don't give out tokens) was probably already dialing 911, but just in case…

When Kyle saw that the booth was empty, despair set in. He then tried his cellphone, but his attempt to call 911 didn't go through.

The second scream was worse. The death cry of a wounded animal, not a man at all. Clearly, it was shirtless guy being hurt. If the cop had lost the upper hand, he would have fired his gun by now.

But the shirtless guy can't die. He said as much. He showed you as much.

The third scream was blood-curdling and set his belly ablaze with fear.

He looked down at his phone as an insane thought hit him: *Imagine if I nut up and go shoot whatever is happening in the tunnel? I could go live on Instagram, catch a cop torturing a guy, and be a hero! Then I won't need a job. I could be an influencer like fucking Ted.*

Ted and Kyle went to high school together. Ted came from a rich family, and had a nice car at sixteen and the entire world at his beck and call. Naturally, Ted was a jerk, then and now. Right out of school, Ted was cast on a reality show for a few years and slept with a bunch of women. Being a televised man-whore should have made him a social pariah. Instead, a body spray company started paying him to be a spokesperson. A body spray company whose core demographic is men who want to be like Ted. Now, he makes almost four-hundred thousand a year after taxes to be a horrible social media troll-person who smells like lavender-scented insect repellent. Kyle hated Ted.

And yet, Ted was definitely on to something. The only difference would be the motivation. Ted needed to be an influencer because he was a narcissistic, unambitious rich person's spawn ill-suited for anything meaningful or beneficial to others. Kyle, while currently motivated by the need for money, could use this moment to become an influencer, but unlike Ted, he'd be an influencer who just happened to be a decent human being.

That meant going down in that tunnel and getting footage of that cop doing horrible things.

Every muscle in both of his legs quivered as he started down the platform, toward the red swinging gate that stood blocking the platform entrance to every subway tunnel in New York City's five boroughs. The gate doubled as a STOP sign, with the words 'Do Not Enter' emblazoned across it. He sighed as he pushed it. The small door squealed from lack of lubricant as he stepped past it. He saw a few tunnel lights in the distance. The light that spilled from the platform threw his shadow long across the small metal staircase leading down into the tunnel. In just a few steps, he plunged into darkness.

He could hear rats scurrying about and screeching but didn't see any as he stepped off the last stair and forced himself to move forward. The ground squished under his weight, and he cursed himself for not remembering that he was in his best dress shoes. Realizing that the damage was done, he shook his head at his own stupidity and pressed on.

Though he was walking in a straight line, he couldn't help but fixate his vision on the one white light he could see. A few more steps and a slight right turn revealed a red signal light that turned green just as he cleared a partition blocking it. He thought about turning on the flashlight app in his cell phone but figured that the cop would see it and either stop torturing the dude or, worse, shoot him.

The actual distance he walked wasn't more than one hundred feet, but in his mind, he might as well have been walking the length of Yankee Stadium.

The strangest noise, a gurgling, made him realize that he'd almost passed them. He turned to see how wrong he'd been about the situation. It had been the cop who was screaming. The shirtless man had in fact gained the advantage on his pursuer in a way that was most unexpected.

The way the shadows were moving, he could tell they were tussling. But even as he opened the phone's video app and aimed it at them, he still couldn't fully make out what was going on. He glanced left to make sure a train wasn't coming before taking another muddy (at least he hoped it was mud) step forward. That's when the phone went into 'low light' mode and automatically switched on the brightest illumination the little minicomputer could muster.

Only now could Kyle see that the tussling he'd been looking at was actually the cop cocooned in an undulating, translucent mass of pink membranes and mucous. His entire body appeared engulfed, save for the top half of his head and his right hand. The lower half of the cop's body was missing, replaced by a cone shaped grouping of particles floating in the living ooze. The particles were disappearing but not without momentarily giving him the appearance of a cartoon genie. In seconds, the particles were gone, dissolved away, leaving just the torso, arms and head. Now that whatever was happening had made some space, the cop's body sank lower into the pink mass.

The cop's gun lay on the ground not three feet away from what was left of him. Inside the trap, his eyes seemed to have lost their lids along with much of the skin that had been on his face minutes ago. His flesh started melting away, merging with and dissolving until it also disappeared.

As flesh gave way to muscle, the cop's uniform, gun belt, and other clothing all seemed to be slipping away and the liquification of the cop's physical form continued. The living mass seemed uninterested in the inorganic matter. Instead of absorbing it as it seemed to be doing with the cop's skin, it shifted the materials away from the body where it quickly ended up in a lower section of the mass and ejected from a hole at the bottom, as if the entity were ridding itself of excrement.

A shaky wrist caused Kyle to involuntarily shine the light further to his right. Now he could see Shirtless Man standing with his head hung low, his arms stretched out like a scarecrow. His mouth gaped open as a trail of the same throbbing, pink translucence protruded out of his face like a hanging tube of salami. Kyle's eyes followed the trail until he saw the connection and realized that the faceless blob ingesting the cop's body was not an independent entity, but an extension of the Shirtless Man's tongue.

Revolted and terrified, Kyle dropped his phone. The harsh video light stayed on. The last thing Kyle would see was the cop's lungs and other internal organs exiting the torso and floating in the ooze, dissolving the way the everything else had.

He turned to run but was tripped up by something after two strides. Something had reached out from the dark and grabbed his ankle. He was suddenly airborne and being carried over the tracks, closer to Shirtless Man and the unorthodox digestive system.

Landing hard on his back, Kyle looked down to see that he had been grabbed by a tentacle that was also part of the monstrous tongue. Frantic, he reached out for something to grab as something slimy eased up into his lower pants leg. Now, he was the one screaming.

Stop!

It was a voice in his head that was not his.

I'm sorry I got you involved. You shouldn't have followed me down here, though. That was dumb.

Kyle's entire body was trembling. "What?!"

This is the result of an experiment. Here, let me show you.

His eyes were forced closed as his mind was flooded with images of a high-end laboratory, the kind you might see in a pharmaceutical ad.

Scientists hired by rich people trying to become immortal. They rewrote my DNA, fused it with different lizard and amphibious animals. They were supposed to kill me, but I got away.

Still subjected to Shirtless Man's point of view, he watched as a white arm that seemed to be coming from his body was jabbed with needles several times. It was difficult to tell how many injections, and if they'd been back-to-back or a series that happened over the course of a few days. Or years.

I am immortal. I can instantly heal from almost anything, but I must feed.

Kyle saw Shirtless Man's first kill, a doctor from the lab dying by giant tongue absorption, pretty much as the cop just had.

They're hunting me. This man I killed was not a real police officer. He worked for them.

Now Kyle was being chased down a long, white corridor. A gun was going off. He turned to see the cop, only he wasn't in a uniform. He was in a suit, firing his weapon, giving off serious henchman vibes.

When I feed, I usually try to find a bad person or wait for someone from the lab to find me. But I was delirious with hunger. That's why I jumped in the tracks. I was trying to kill myself. But I can't die.

The scene Kyle saw from the safety of the platform now played out in his head as if he were the one jumping into the tracks and trying to decapitate himself with an express train. As he lay down and the train approached, things went black for a moment, then he was back on his feet, climbing back up to the platform and running up to...

"Me."

My need to feed is unbearable, indescribable misery that I can't suppress, otherwise I would just starve myself.

"You were going to eat me."

I was. My thought was that no one would miss this random, skinny black kid. But then I realized that was wrong. Plus, I could sense the goon coming into the station, so I let you go. Then I went to the tunnel and waited.

"But how did you know…?"

I secrete a residue. It's invisible to the naked eye but comes up a bright green for anyone wearing contact lenses the lab gives its security goons for the purposes of being able to track us if we get away.

"We?"

Yes. There were more than just me in the lab. And I am not the only one who escaped, and this man is not the only tracker. You are going to run home and completely clean your clothes so they don't think you're one of us.

"Jesus!"

I'm going to let you go now. During our connection, I gleaned why you came down here, but I'm not sure you want these people to know who you are. While it would be a help to me, you could very well get yourself in a world of trouble. You better delete the footage and forget about this.

As Kyle regained control of his eyes, the cold sliminess and the grip on his leg slipped away. He sat up and turned. The Shirtless Man was gone. There was nothing left to account for what had happened to him but his ruined suit and shoes. Behind him, the train pulled into the tunnel.

On the train that arrived some minutes after that one, his fellow commuters gave him a wide berth. Most averted their eyes, but there were some looks of sympathy. When he got home, he changed into some sweats then put the job interview outfit into a plastic bag and took them to the incinerator. Alone in his apartment, his eyes found his cellphone that he'd thrown carelessly on the bed when he was changing. He thought about looking at the footage before he realized he had a voicemail:

Hey, Kyle! This is Yuri from Kaleidoscope. I was hoping to catch you before you left out. I actually have to postpone your interview. My wife went into labor a month earlier than we expected, so I am actually leaving the office now. Give me a call tomorrow and we can reschedule. Really sorry about this. I hope you don't get all the way here before you get this message. Okay, take care.

Kyle chuckled and shook his head. Still staring down at the phone, he finally hit PLAY and watched the footage until it went black. Since he had dropped it mid-incident, he wasn't sure it had all recorded. But he could hear his own voice responding to what the thing from the subway had said to him via its cold, telepathic tentacle. The last thing he saw was his own face, dimly lit but nonetheless clearly frightened. As the events replayed in his head, he thought long and hard about posting the footage to his social media. Then, he closed his eyes and saw a different vision. Men dressed in black, bursting into his apartment. Their guns were drawn, all pointed at him as if they were capturing some mass murderer. He saw himself being shot multiple times, his life fading further away with each bloody eruption in his chest.

Saddened by his own lack of bravery, he hit the DELETE button and tossed the phone onto the bed.

The Edge of Mercy
A Tale of Altiva
Teel James Glenn

The young Kovar priest hunched forward on the neck of his mount and strained his eyes against the wind and the darkness in search of his prey. Somewhere in the night, a wild tvek pack howled their whistling night cry and sent a chill up the priest's spine.

We are all hunting, he thought to the savage reptiles, *but those I hunt will wish you had found them instead when my work is done.*

The priest urged the antlered war vorn he rode to greater speed despite the darkness and a narrow trail. At times, his drawn crystal sword would strike an outcropping of rock, producing a bell chime, or the branching antler of the vorn would scrape against the mountain wall and elicit a *bleat* of protest from the beast.

"Easy, Windracer," the priest said in a tortured whisper. "Just a little longer. The oil merchant they robbed said they were only an hour gone." There was urgency in his rasped voice that seemed to both calm and inspire the vorn, and it pressed ahead with renewed purpose.

Lord Erique Shoutte, priest of the Kovar, gripped the reins in one hand and his curved crystal blade Vengeancefang in the other. *The last ones*, he thought, his slate grey eyes raking the blackness. *Myrran can rest after this night.*

He urged his mount to even more reckless speed, his face pressed almost into the beast's mane to avoid the cutting mountain wind.

Man and beast rounded a fold in the cliff face just as the two moons peeked momentarily through the dense cloud cover to reveal an ambush. A mounted rider holding a torch blocked the road ahead in front of the stolen, oil-laden cart. Above the trail, Shoutte was able to see two men perched on ledges above and to the right of the trail.

I am supposed to see your flame and lose my night vision to see your friends, eh, rider, Shoutte thought with an evil smile. *Not so, by the Rythem!*

Shoutte kicked his mount into a charge at the instant the two bandits above leapt for him. Vengeancefang arced up, slicing one man cleanly from armpit to neck, but the second man landed square on the priest's back.

The bandit got a strangling arm around Shoutte's throat and tried an overhand stab, but Shoutte was able to parry with his crystal sword, locking both weapons.

Shoutte's vorn shied at the sudden weight then charged on, partially blinded by the spray of gore from the airborne bandit. The vorn rammed head on into Torch Bearer's mount, sending both animals and their riders pitching sideways in a tangle of arms, legs, and antlers.

The five bodies seemed to freeze for an eternal moment before slamming into the blue shale of the path's edge that gave way to a shower of loose pebbles.

Lord Shoutte had the impression of the ground heaving up at him and vaguely sensed that the cart had somehow become entangled in the tumbling mass before the confusion and the blinding pain overwhelmed him and all was black.

First, his mind woke up.

There was a vague awareness of being that lasted for a long time. Then he knew blackness existed and it swarmed in on him from all sides. With the awareness came memory and a face carved of ivory with emerald eyes that pierced him.

Then there was sensation: Heat! He could feel it on his face, feel the sweat that dripped corrosively down his cheeks. He thought of movement, compelling his right arm to lift. Sudden agony forced him to abandon the attempt and for a long time, he lay breathing heavily from the exertion and the pain.

He became conscious of sound in the darkness beyond his closed eyelids and a wind that slapped at him with icy hands, causing him to alternately shiver and perspire. He became aware of a dull ache in his left leg. An abortive attempt to move it proved to him it was injured in some way. He had to clench his teeth to keep down his gorge.

Shoutte opened his eyes, flickering the lids to clear them of perspiration, and felt himself panicking; everything was velvet black.

I'm blind! he thought. A knot of fear forced itself up his throat. He remembered the time and, by staring hard enough, was able to make out the tiny blue-white pinholes in the velvet.

Lord Shoutte realized after some thought that he was on his back facing out toward a night sky. *Be at ease, Erique*, he ordered himself in a hoarse whisper. *Find the Rhythm—reason it out.* He slowly turned his head to the left.

The hard black ground suddenly became blacker five feet from where he was lying, and from the sound of the wind that howled beyond the darkness, he was sure he'd landed at the edge of a cliff.

Gritting his teeth, the priest shifted his gaze downward, lifting his head away from the cold stone. He could see past the skill brand on his chest and his sword girdle to thighs, shadowed by an outcropping of rock.

His left arm was stretched out, palm up, away from his body, almost at the edge of the greater darkness. Tentative movement of the fingers brought no appreciable pain, so he flexed the whole hand. He anticipated agony but raised the arm until it was overhead. There was no pain.

He stared at his hand with delight. Gradually, he became aware that the right side of the hand was more sharply defined. He turned his head to the right. There was a gentle upward incline abruptly sliced by a barrier of light: fire. The low flames ran in a line parallel to his body and perpendicular to the rise of the incline for fifteen feet, fed by dry bush and a black liquid that gleamed in the flickering light.

Beyond the flaming wall...the night!

A sudden stab of pain brought his thoughts back to himself. His right arm, twisted beneath him, seared with pain.

Within the pain, he was aware of a new surge of heat that coursed through him. Heat not caused by the wall of flame; heat mindless of the chilling wind that buffeted him.

Fever, he realized. *I will be with you soon, Myrran*, he thought with an attempted smile. *My work is done.*

Shoutte had trained as a healer and knew he would soon die of exposure if he was not found. There was little chance of a search party locating him in the maze of mountain trails. Few would venture beyond the safety of a village stockade after moons-rise with wild tvek packs running loose.

The priest sighed with relief, with the certain knowledge that a two-year odyssey of vengeance was at an end. He would at last be with his beloved contract-wife Myrran.

"Help!" The voice off to Shoutte's right was faint and desperate. "Help me!"

Shoutte turned his head with effort and strained his eyes. Gradually, the shadowy bulk of a dead vorn became clear. It was lying on its side at the very edge of the precipice, its head lolling at an odd angle.

Beneath the vorn was another shape—an indistinct form that, as Shoutte stared at it, began to move in short, jerky motions. And moan. "Help me! My legs are trapped beneath this beast!"

Shoutte's first thought was to crawl to the man's assistance, but then his mind went ablaze with the image of Myrran lying dead at his feet, gutted like a slaughtered svor, and he had but one thought: *One of them who killed Myrran is more alive than I can bear.*

Lord Erique Shoutte bolted upright at the crystal smith's table and squeezed the tankard of ale before him as if to wring the life from it. He had hardly touched his food and spent most of the meal with his slate grey eyes fixed on a memory.

"What can be done, priest-son?" the smith said in a voice that chimed. "My daughter, your contract-wife, is these three moons-cycles dead. You yourself said there may have been a dozen of the bandits."

"A dozen or a hundred, by the Rythem," Shoutte croaked in a pained whisper, "I will find each and make their transitions as agonizing as possible." Barely a man, Erique Shoutte had aged a lifetime in three months.

His black mane of hair which hung to his shoulders was now flecked with gray. The lines around his mouth, which were once laugh lines, had become shadows of tension. The most visible change of all was the jagged pink scar which cut across the front of his throat like a hideous necklace.

The bandit who had cut his throat had scarred the Kovar priest inside as well. "I want your craft, Mastersmith, I want you to grow a crystal sword for me."

"You would give your blood to have their blood?" the crystal smith asked, entwining his frail, bony fingers. "You would perhaps give your life futilely?"

"I will not die in the process," Shoutte said, not with the arrogance of youth, but the certainty of a zealot. "I did not survive the knife, suture my wound, and heal myself to die at a leeching."

"Others, stronger and more purposed than even you, have died blooding a crystal sword," the smith said. "I have made but five such weapons and attempted three others. Two died and the third nearly so before he wisely stopped the process." The smith was standing beside the priest now and placed a hand on Shoutte's shoulder. "I have lost my only daughter, Erique, must I lose my acquired son to this senselessness?"

Shoutte looked into the old man's eyes and for a moment saw the child in the parent. "I must do this, father, and if you will not help me, I will go elsewhere."

The smith stared at him and knew he could not be dissuaded.

"You will wish to begin immediately, I take it?" There was a hint of amusement in the older man's voice.

"Yes."

"Then eat all that is on your plate while I fetch you more. We must begin building your strength."

The smith turned away to go to the hearth and added, "It will take me three weeks to prepare the necessary chemicals, barely long enough to prepare your body and mind for what must come."

Lord Shoutte watched the crystal smith and reflected on his words. "Three weeks to prepare the solution, three months since...Myrran, and thirty days to grow the sword. Three, three and three again; it is an Omphast omen. A good portend."

The Omphast was the symbol of the Kovar religion. Shoutte had an Omphast branded on the center of his chest as a mark of his priesthood, one diamond brand at the end of each three-year phase of study as chanter ("never again"), healer ("of what use save to prolong my life?") and warrior ("avenger").

"Now I have an Omphast burned into my soul as well."

Just then, the crackling of the fire seemed to intensify as if to echo his inner flame, but with a derogatory hiss.

The suddenly brighter light revealed more of the features of the trapped bandit. He was a small man, perhaps frail, with a face that, had it not been twisted in pain, might have been termed delicate and worthy of pity.

Lord Shoutte's thoughts did not run to pity, however. He thought only of his sword. *Vengeancefang shall drink one more time before I rest,* he thought. *But where is it?* Shoutte forced himself to relax his mental focus so he could 'feel' his crystal sword in his mind.

Everything went hazy, then he felt himself warming up and his eyes focused again. He was cold but the strength-stealing chills had passed. *There, beyond the fire,* he thought. *I must get to Vengeancefang.* He ignored the continuous moans from the bandit.

Shoutte moved his good hand slowly over the ground until he found a small scrub bush. Digging his heel into a hollow in the rock face of the incline, he arched his back, raising himself off his right forearm. He was careful to avoid moving the arm, but the edge of the cliff to his left was also in his mind.

He dropped to the ground, winded. The arm was bent oddly beside instead of beneath him. Blood from his lip, where he had dug his teeth in, dribbled warmly to his chin.

Good; I must make a plan and adhere to it. He glanced up the incline at the slow burning wall of fire. *The hand first, by the Rythem."*

He inched his left hand across his body until he had a firm grip on a belt pouch from which he pulled out his kerchief.

"Onward, Erique boy. You are not defeated until you are dead and you are not dead until you don't know it!" It sounded funny for the words to be coming from so sprightly a form as Arinna, funnier still that the tiny girl should be driving the broad-shouldered Erique Shoutte backwards across the exercise yard with her sword blows. Funny to everyone in the yard but Erique.

Shoutte had received his priest singer and healer skill brands but was only half way to his warrior brand. Arinna was the temple school sword master's daughter. Master Braphon had often quoted the Warrior's Creed to Shoutte as he had forced him across the yard but had just as often called him "my second-best pupil."

Arinna was his best.

"Keep your guard up, Erique!" The teenage girl teased as she lunged at Shoutte's belly.

Shoutte barely parried to riposte at her head with a wide two-handed stroke.

The girl parried steel to steel, but Shoutte suddenly shifted his weight and, still keeping his blade in contact with hers, slid forward with a pommel strike to her head.

Arinna abruptly sat down.

"Are you all right, little one?" Shoutte asked, examining the already growing lump on the girl's forehead.

"Oh, of course," she grumped. "I've given and taken worse." Nonetheless, she accepted Shoutte's aid in standing and walking to the shade and water bucket.

"A good morning's exercise," Master Braphon commented as he walked past the two youngsters on his way out to the yard. He often watched morning free practice from his study's window.

"A good strike," he murmured as he made a quick examination of Arinna's head. "Doubt if it will knock any sense into you, though." He smiled at her grimace and moved out into the yard.

In his hand was Wickcutter, his crystal sword. Master Braphon strode with a relaxed yet purposeful gait to the center pit of the yard, greeting students and instructors as he went. Once at the practice pit, he removed his outer robe to reveal his triple branded barrel chest and massive sword-scarred arms.

All eyes in the yard turned toward the center pit. All practice stopped when Master Braphon drew Wickcutter. All ears listened to the melodic chime as the priest-swordsman tapped the grown crystal sword against a carved crystal scabbard to begin his solo practice form.

Shoutte, along with everyone who viewed the Master, was mesmerized by the angular precision of Wickcutter's strokes. With scabbard in one hand, the Master leapt, spun, kicked, cut, lunged, and parried for almost half an hour, moving with the grace of a man half his size and age.

The clear, crystal blade whistled through the air, almost singing a truth chant with its pitches and tones. The entire man was focused through the blade, focused yet relaxed. Not a single movement was hurried or forced.

"He raises the way of the warrior to an art form," Shoutte said reverently to Arinna. "To watch him attack and defend against so many."

The girl smiled. "He fights only one," the Master's daughter said. "It is his greed he defends from and his vice through which he lunges."

"I don't understand," Shoutte said with puzzlement.

Arinna smiled, shook her head, and clucked at the older man as if he were the child, then whacked Shoutte across the knuckles of his hand.

"Perhaps that will knock some sense into you."

Shoutte's fingers were numb from the cold and it took him a long time to knot one end of the kerchief through his belt. The other end he passed beneath his right arm and tied to his waist.

With the arm resting on his stomach like part of a broken toy, Shoutte grabbed hold of a nearby bush and maneuvered in stages toward the wall of fire.

When he reached the bush, Shoutte abandoned it for a rock further up the incline. His fingertips were bloodied from the grating of the coarse rock, and his left arm felt as if it would wrench itself from the socket with every inch of progress. The goal was the sword, but he blocked all thought of what he would do when he got there and pushed aside the notion that he might not have the strength to reach the trapped bandit. For the moment, it was enough that there was a goal.

Shoutte's left leg was in constant pain, a now dull, now sharp pain that he put out of his mind. The rough ground clawed at his back, tearing the fabric of his tunic and shirt to shreds so that soon, rock tore into his naked back.

The crackling of fire above him, the howl of the wind, and the moans of the bandit below him filled Shoutte's consciousness to the exclusion of all else until a new sound imposed itself. It was a series of high-pitched whistles or trills followed by a clucking sound.

Shoutte realized he had been hearing it for some time, but now the calls were getting noticeably louder and nearer.

Calls. The hunting calls of a pack of wild tveks.

They have our scent, Shoutte thought, *I must hasten to Vengancefang lest their hunger cheats me of my revenge.* He redoubled his speed in pushing toward the wall of flame and tried to ignore all but his inner ache.

At last he lay with the heat of live flame only a few feet away, his chest heaving, his hand raw and painful. The fire had died somewhat, having used up the last burning brush. In the dancing shadows, the priest could make out the oil jar that had ruptured when the vorns had tumbled off the trail. It was the base fuel for the fire. It would burn for more time than he could afford.

Near the wall of flame he could see several unbroken jars of oil, still sealed on their sides. Eventually the heat might rupture them and add to the fire, but Shoutte thought grimly, *I shall have made my transition to the next life by then.*

The sword lay beyond, near the road. He knew that the heat from the fire might keep him alive longer, but he was blocked from the sword by a rise in the ground. The space on either side of the barrier was too narrow for him to pull himself through, and even so it was over eight feet to the sword.

Damned if I do and damned if I don't, he thought. He stared up at the indifferent stars until tears blurred their crisp, white light.

He came to himself with an angry snarl. "Damn stupid," he said. "I shall not do that." The pain from his arm made him wince and cry out in surprise. "Good," he grunted, "that will keep my head." By shimmying his body, he knocked his right arm against a protrusion of rock. He screamed with the pain but it brought a lucid flow of adrenalin.

"Onward, you bastard son of a tvek," he grunted through clenched teeth. "Get up to Vengeancefang before you're tvek food." He started to push with his one good foot, squirming.

When he came to the rise of stone, he kicked hard with his heel, skidding it along the rough stone below him and scraping his back raw on the gravel. The action forced him halfway past the twin walls of fire, smothering the flame beneath him, but it used his last ounce of strength.

He collapsed.

Then the chills returned.

The sweat blinded him when he tried to see. The fire on each side of him singed his arm when he squirmed from the pain and the fever. The stone bit deep into his back. All the blue-white stars turned fire red and began to swirl and eddy around him. Some darted close to sear his skin while others maintained a disdainful aloofness and mocked him with soundless laughter.

The fire.

The pain!

The memories.

HER GREEN EYES STARING AT HIM, LOOKING THROUGH HIM.

Shoutte felt a surge of strength pour through him when his fingers wrapped around the carved agate, serpentine handle of Vengeancefang.

"It is beautiful, Master Smith," Shoutte whispered weakly. "Truly magnificent." Then the young priest sighed and lowered his arm to the sleeping pallet on which he had lain for 26 days.

"The blade is almost fully formed," the smith said. He set aside the intricately carved handle he had made to fit on the crystal blade. "I thought the feathered dragon of your family crest would be an apt motif."

Shoutte looked at the hilt again: it was shaped like a feathered snake, its tail curled around the grip at the base and its body wrapped in a wide spiral around the grip to act as knuckle guards. Its reptilian jaws gaped wide and appeared to swallow a blue-green jewel that would act as pommel stone.

"There will be no sword like it in all of Altiva," Shoutte whispered with awe.

"Just so," the smith said, "the idea came to me in a dream, and gods do not often make such gifts." Then his manner changed from artist to strictly business. "Now, I must bleed you again. The solution grows weak."

Shoutte steeled himself, focusing his mind on the mantra for strength that had helped sustain him through the daily bloodlettings. He had watched the pool of liquid in the crystal dish beside him bubble and hiss as his life essence was added to it, and felt the growth of the blade in his mind. It was like growing a new limb—strange yet familiar.

In a short time, he would have the herbal broth that had strengthened him physically during the bleedings, which had replenished and thickened his blood for the growing.

Shoutte focused on and through the blade of Vengeancefang. He enjoyed the cool efficiency of the curve, the geometric perfection of its point, and the crystalline inevitability of the razor sharp edge. The hilt's rough texture was security for Shoutte, and the carved feathers soothed rather than hurt his braised palm.

He lay a long time, catching his breath and savoring the cool agate in his left hand.

I have but to reach the bandit and I can die, he thought.

"*Aroooo cluck cluck!*" The tvek call was only a few feet away in the darkness. And it was answered: "*Aroo cluck*

cluck!" Soon the night air was full of the whistle-clucks and the salivatory hisses of the tvek pack.

Shoutte could see perhaps half a dozen sets of feral red eyes reflecting the fire out of the darkness and slowly advancing on him.

Shoutte knew he could not squirm away from them fast enough.

With a sudden jolt of horror, he realized that the path his body had made through the flames would lead the tveks directly to the wounded bandit.

His wounded bandit.

"No!" He rasped and flung his sword arm across his body violently so that it caused him to begin to roll sideways down the embankment, through the flames and toward the vorn carcass that pinned the bandit.

He moved like a log rolling down a hill, but this log screamed in agony every time it rolled over its right arm. Somewhere on the way down, it occurred to Shoutte through the shards of blinding white pain that he might overshoot the bandit and fly off into space, but there was little he could do about it. Momentum and pain made it impossible to stop until he slammed into the dead vorn and all but blacked out.

"Must stay awake long enough—" Shoutte tried to force himself upright, but he had come to a stop resting face down on his bad arm. Somehow, he managed to retain hold of Vengeancefang, but he lay in a semi-delirious state trying to remember why he hurt so much.

So tired, Shoutte thought, *maybe if I sleep the pain will go away*. Suddenly, nothing mattered more than resting. Resting perhaps forever.

"Ow!" Something bit Shoutte on the right calf. A second adrenal surge of pain brought the present into razor alertness. He kicked back with his leg but whatever was biting him would not let go.

"Let me die in peace!" He tried to roll over, but there was another tug at his leg and a reptilian hiss. *A tvek*, Shoutte thought with horrified clarity. *I'm being eaten alive by a tvek!*

Suddenly Shoutte raged with explosive force. "How dare you!" The priest yanked his leg free from the jaws, rolled his body over, and slashed down.

The almost man-sized reptile looked up at Shoutte with an indignant expression as it munched on flesh from Shoutte's leg. It made a strangled hissing sound as Vengeancefang sliced through the upper beak, almost severing it, and scurried away in pain.

The pack was through the flames now, closing in for an easy kill. Or so they thought.

Shoutte used his crystal sword to pull himself up to one knee and put his back to the dead vorn.

"Help me, please," the bandit behind Shoutte moaned. "Don't let them get me."

Shoutte spared the second to look down at the trapped man.

The bandit's eyes were glazed over from pain and he obviously had no clear idea who Shoutte was. The bandit and the vorn above him were coated in some of the oil from the merchant's cart. Only a fortunate fluke had caused the lit torch to fall at the higher oil spill.

Then all time for reflection was past and Shoutte faced the winter-starved animal pack at butcher's work. At first, they attacked in groups of two or three, hissing and clucking in slow stalks, but Vengeancefang's arc was wider than they expected.

Three fell dead.

The tveks backed off for a moment, then charged at full speed in ones and twos to fall victim to the deadly accurate left-handed slash of the crystal blade. The sinewy, iridescent-green bodies hurled themselves with suicidal fury at the priest until they were piled waist deep around him and there were only three of them left.

An Omphast omen, Shoutte thought bitterly. His sword arm hung limp at his side, the muscles so far beyond pain and exhaustion that it was a thing apart from him that functioned on an imperative of its own.

And all the while the trapped bandit recited his litany of pain and terror in a monotone. "Please don't let them kill me. I hurt so much. So much. I don't want to die. Please, I don't want to die..."

The three lizards fanned out and moved to the outer limit of Vengeancefang's arc. They allowed Shoutte time enough for one thought before their final attack.

I should do what must be done with the bandit, Shoutte thought, *and let these creatures send me in transition. It would be faster.*

When the three attacked, though, Shoutte's instinct for survival called Vengeancefang into play.

The first was smashed in mid-air by the flat of the blade and sent flying over the precipice.

The second, he cleanly decapitated so that the body fell with an obscene thump onto the antlers of the vorn, frozen in a grotesque parody of a leap.

The last tvek survived one slashing cut that severed one paw and attempted to retreat, but Shoutte swung wildly and struck it on the rump with the false edge of the blade. This knocked the creature further off balance so that as it attempted to escape up the incline, it careened into the pile of oil jars, smashing some of them.

Shoutte watched with a sense of unreal horror as the oil from the jars oozed into two streams, one coming down the hill in a black wave and one moving straight for the fire as if magnetically drawn to it.

In seconds, the flaming wall charged toward Shoutte.

Even the semi-conscious bandit felt the heat and saw the blaze moving toward him and realized what was happening.

"Don't let me burn," the litany became. "Don't let me burn!" The man seemed to gain a sudden lucidity from his fear and his eyes focused on Shoutte. Eyes which, in the suddenly bright light of the fire, Shoutte could see were emerald green. "Please, don't let me burn."

The exhausted priest had only a moment to choose between the blade and the flame. He stared into the pleading green eyes and chose the blade.

Vengeancefang cut cleanly through the bandit's neck. The green eyes were forever sightless and forever open. Forever pleading.

Shoutte half crawled, half fell away from the bodies as the flames swept over the bandit, vorn, and tveks with an explosive *whoosh*!

The flame singed the hair of the priest, and the cooked flesh smell made him nauseous. For a long time, he could not stop staring at the burning skull of the bandit, his mind's eye superimposing the pleading emerald eyes.

Then he looked down at the crystal sword in his hand and began to cry. The sword he had grown for holy vengeance had killed the last of the murderers of his wife, but it was not an act of vengeance. Not even an act of justice.

"Mercy," Shoutte whispered. "I killed him as an act of mercy."

He took the crystal sword and, with a whimpered cry, hurled the blade out over the cliff. "I want to die!" The priest collapsed at last, falling on his back.

Out in the darkness the crystal sword whistled like a siren as the mountain winds buffeted it. Then somewhere below, the hand of the wind slammed the sword against the mountainside and the sword chimed. It toppled down the mountainside, sliding and tumbling, resonating each time it struck the rock. The cacophonous symphony was echoed by the far slopes and rolled back in waves to pound the priest's consciousness.

I'm sorry, Myrran, Shoutte thought, *to be so weak I could not make true my promise to you.*

And from out of the darkness, the echoed chiming of the falling sword rang louder like a temple knell of death.

"Forgive me, Myrran," Shoutte whispered, "I seem to have made a mess of it." He looked at the pie dough he had been rolling and shrugged. "I must have left something out."

Myrran Yar Sen smiled her world-warming smile and looked down at the doughy monster in front of Shoutte. "Flour, Erique," she corrected. "Add more flour. Why is it you always overlook the simple things?"

"But you are such a simple maid," Shoutte replied in his deep bass voice. "How is it I did not overlook you?" His smile was sweet and mischievous.

He was still smiling when the handful of flour hit him in the face. A glob of dough was retaliation and soon the two of them, giggling like school children, had made a mess of themselves and the kitchen.

"You are a crazy wench," Shoutte laughed, clearing egg batter off his face. "I think my duty as a priest of the

Kovar should be to protect the world from your madness."

"And how will you do that?" She tried to remove a lump of dough from her fire red hair, but grew frustrated and gave up in favor of picking salad out of her bodice.

"I shall have to make you my contract-wife for life," Shoutte said, suddenly serious, "if you will have me?"

Myrran stared at him for a long moment with a neutral expression on her face, then said in a quiet whisper, "Of course I'll have you, you crazy priest. Who else would want you?"

An embrace he would never forget.

"It could be a hard life being the wife of a Kovar priest," Shoutte said. "My duties will call me so often."

"I can help."

"You will not always be able to."

"I have always helped my father," she smiled. "He has even said I'm quite bright."

"There will be danger."

"Are you trying to back out of our marriage so soon?"

"No."

"Sometimes I think you use the Kovar as an excuse to never make up your mind."

"It's just that no circumstance is eternal, no truth is forever," Shoutte said solemnly, "no matter how much we want them to be."

"There are some things inexorably true, so true, so In-the-Rythem that they can be incontrovertibly almost forever." She smiled and ran the fingers of one hand lightly across Shoutte's throat. "Forever like our love."

He looked at her kneeling on the messy kitchen floor covered with half the kitchen's contents and thought, *She should look like a scarecrow, yet she shines like an Umbrian goddess of beauty. Such a beauty is from inside and must surely last.*"

"Come back, my paladin priest," Myrran whispered, "your thoughts are so far away from me."

"It is just that we must always be willing to change our paths. The choices are so many."

Outside, the temple bells chimed evening prayers.

"As long as you always choose for the Rythem, for the truth, Erique," she whispered, "our paths will always be together."

The crystal chimes faded away into the crisp night air and Lord Shoutte had one last thought.

I travel your path tonight, my love, forever.

Then the black of the night overwhelmed him and he was content.

It was a surprise to Lord Shoutte when he woke up and found himself still among the living. He was on a sleeping pallet in a healer's shack and his hands, right arm, back, and right calf were extensively bandaged. He was not, however, in pain.

"I gave you a strong broth of thodist leaves," the healer said, "during one of your more lucid moments. It has lulled your nerves to sleep."

"How long have I been here?" the priest asked.

"Fully nine days," the healer said. "An oil merchant from Kwor brought you to me."

"How did he find me in the mountains?" Shoutte asked.

"This." The healer held up Shoutte's crystal sword in its scabbard and set it on the pallet beside the priest. "The merchant said he had no idea where you were, and he and a search party had given up looking when, he said, 'a sound like temple bells' called him to the spot where the sword had fallen. He found you above it."

Shoutte meekly stroked the agate handle and smiled.

"I am curious to know your name," the healer asked, "and the name of so unusual a sword."

"I am Lord Erique Shoutte, of Umbria, priest of the Kovar," Shoutte said with renewed pride. "And this is my sword, Rythemwand, named by my forever-wife Myrran."

The healer did not understand why Shoutte began to cry then, but concluded it was the ordeal, and so left man and sword alone to rest.

Whistleblower

Hunter C. Eden

My grandfather was a student at Columbine High School
when Eric Harris and Dylan Klebold went on their
rampage. He didn't know them. He didn't see them the
day it happened. He just heard the gunshots. Afterwards,
everybody argued whether it was bullying or mental
illness or guns or video games or rock music; my
grandfather didn't know any better than anyone else.
Seventy-eight years later, nobody does. But I know why
little Jimmy Madison just murdered seven kids in his first-
grade class with a kitchen knife.

We called *Collage d'Infant* "eduneering." A custom-
made VR set shows babies and pre-verbal toddlers in a
series of random objects and places. For thirty seconds,
the kid sits on a virtual seashore. The warm sand, the cool
spray, the salty smell. *Collage d'Infant* made it all real.
Baby's first trip to the beach. For the next thirty seconds,
the kid holds an apple. The red, waxy skin, the sweet
crunch...to baby's little mind, it's a real apple in every
way except existence. Picked and curated by a carefully
selected board of pediatric psychiatrists, the images create
certain associations that have deep subconscious

resonance for the growing child, stimulating them to embark on a lifetime journey of knowledge. And what could be bad about that?

The senior management at Braina Vista, Inc. thought it was a great idea, so we made a few calls, got some academics to sign off on the basic premise that what happens to us as children affects us as adults, got drunk, and made a big spreadsheet with a list of things we figured kids would like. Nothing violent or crazy or sexual—just random, harmless shit like beaches and apples and playing with bears and flying through the stars. Two years of programming and engineering later, we had *Collage d'Infant*. Is that even French? All the international editions had different distributors, so I don't know what they call it over there.

We released it on October 1st, 2071. Black Friday that year saw multiple hospitalizations as throngs of helicopter parents brawled in toy store aisles for the last box on the shelves. You can't put your child on the track to success and achievement too soon, and if that means curb-stomping some granola mom who drove all the way from Spokane, well, Little Timmy/Julie will thank you when Harvard sends its acceptance letter. Oh, you're *not* buying *Collage* for Junior? It's okay. Maybe scrubbing toilets will be a very rewarding career.

Collage d'Infant outsold every other early childhood education tool on the market. It wasn't even close. If your kid wasn't hooked up with a *Collage* set, they might as well have been playing with blocks. The market was there. What we needed was some really good premium content we could release just in time for next Christmas. So we came up with Professor Baby—a virtual playmate and teacher to help your baby on the road to lifelong learning—*and fun!!!*

Professor Baby's design was extremely creative: a Chibi baby in professor clothes. We had to go back and forth with the design team, because nobody wants their baby's *Collage d'Infant* experience curated by Professor Adorable Cancer Patient, but we finally got a big-headed gender-neutral baby in a diaper, wearing a mortarboard. Fuck you, "it's not original." What, is little Kwan lying in his crib doing a sophisticated critique of cartoon baby characters in modern American media? Of course not. The only way to stimulate abstract critical thinking skills like that so early is through *Collage d'Infant*'s premium content.

Let Professor Baby sing to your child's developing brain about continents or flowers or how we brush our teeth or cows going *moo* and dogs going *bow wow*. We're having a Cyber Monday special on lifetime subscriptions. You don't think $200,000 is too much to set your child up for lifelong learning, do you? We have payment plans with great interest rates for those whose economic means don't match their educational dreams, so why not give your growing child the gift of Professor Baby's top-tier content? Only an abusive, neglectful monster and probable pedophile would deny their child such a golden opportunity for success.

And then, four years after *Collage d'Infant* hit the market and three years after we debuted Professor Baby, it began. Five-year old Martin Sylvan clipped his friend's throat with a loppers. No reason. He just did it, the same way four-year old Billy Donegan stabbed the girl down the street to death with a screwdriver before going home and burying it in his mother's stomach. No reason. And lest you think this was just white boy toxic masculinity, remember little Suzy Yao, who threw her baby brother out a fifth story window, and Tamika Washington, who used a glass paperweight from her dad's office to bash her sleeping grandmother's head in. No reason for her or any of the other 91,873 verified incidents we've logged, 96.4% of which involved registered users of *Collage d'Infant*, with 73.7% in the premium subscriber tier.

Circumstantial evidence, we said. *Collage d'Infant* is a very popular product. I'm sure 96.4% of those households drank coffee or used anti-bacterial soap. We tested it on rats, just to have some good hard data to counter the fearmongering. We didn't get that from rats. Or dogs. Or chimps. Breaking this stuff down into data and algorithms is antiseptic. But looking at the blood in the cages, hearing those shrieks, I knew I was done.

I don't know *why*, is the fucking thing. It was all just random pictures and a cartoon baby singing about how five little elephants were learning how to dance, one fell over and ripped his pants, four little elephants, etc. etc. That was literally it. We don't know if those 91,873 were susceptible to something and the rest will grow up to be everything we promised in the advertisement. Maybe they will. Or maybe, as their brains continue to develop, we'll see 90,000 more incidents as they reach their tween years. And 90,000 more when those adolescent hormones really hit. Our brains keep developing until the age of twenty-five. What does that look like for the *Collage d'Infant* generation?

That's why I'm sending you the attached videos and data from the tests we ran. I've also included engineering specs for Braina Vista's next big product, the most exciting offering in the *Collage d'Infant* suite yet. *Classwomb: Collage d'Infant In Utero.*™

Never too early to set them up for success, right?

It Closes the Eye of the Sun

Daniel Arthur Smith

The wooden wagons camped beneath a calm sky of small, pillowy, white clouds, each brilliantly outlined in gold, with grand rays beaming down between them onto the endless surrounding plains. As the wagons settled in the trail boss, an old soldier who went by Captain Elias visited each of two dozen small buffalo chip fires to check on those gathered around them: a mix of families from European countries he'd only heard of, pioneers whom mere months before had emigrated by ship from the old world to claim the free land promised in Oregon. They had left the Texas territory with more, but crossing the rivers had taken six wagons and as many settlers, unable to swim, drowned in the current. Along the trail, snakes and dysentery had robbed families of fathers and mothers and children. The faces of those left circled around the small fires were gaunt and worn, their eyes dark and sunken. At the last of the day, the clouds darkened to indigo and the rays beaming down between them grew brighter. A settler, a German named Gunther, commented to Elias in broken English that the bright beams were *God's rays*, that they were good luck—the old soldier knew better.

The night that followed was without stars and, with the exception of intermittent rumbling of far-off thunder, deathly quiet.

Elias gathered with the men he'd hired to help drive the train, most old soldiers themselves, by the light of his fire. Their conversation was nil as they too knew what loomed in the dark.

"We should go now," the cookie warned. "Break camp and push toward the Fort."

A long rolling rumble of distant thunder filled the gap between words.

Elias rolled his eyes, but it was his second, Randall who responded to the nervous cook. "Four of those wagons are just women and children," he said. "They'd have a hard time breaking camp at night."

"As most all of them would," added Elias. "They're still green to the country."

The cook scowled, then said, "But you know what hides in the storm. Bandits, rustlers… and other unspeakable things."

"Unspeakable things?" asked Dandrich, a Texan cowboy hired to move the small herd of cattle behind the train. "What kind of unspeakable things?"

Elden, a Comanche guide and the youngest among them, spoke up. "My people say the storm god comes to chase those from the land who would steal from it. He rides an evil spirit through the skies, the great thunder bird Hurakan. He comes swiftly through the air in the shape of a giant blue cloud, a cloud so large it closes the eye of the sun and makes the land in front of him dark. Then the wind begins to blow, first here, then there. Then the wind grows strong and howls as the god and his thunder bird come flying through the sky."

"For real?" asked Dandrich.

"It's a story kid," said Randall. "Hurakan is just a way to explain hurricanes and they only happen in the water and on the coast."

"Yes," said Elden. "The storm god used to chase others from our land when we lived by the water. But now this land is Comanche land, and he brings his demons to rid this land of invaders."

Elias watched the faces of his riders, all but Randall open mouthed and hanging on the young Comanche's words. "Okay," he said. "That's enough of that. The storms a comin' and there's not much we can do about it jawing tonight. Best we get what rest we can. We move at first light and hope for the best."

First light delivered a massive indigo discus cloud spanning the expansive southern horizon as high as the mountains to the west, and beneath it a wide, towering column of rain. The shadow of the storm tinted the white canvas coverings of the schooners and the grasses of the plains an ominous gunmetal grey. Not many in the wagons had witnessed such a sight—the old world they'd fled was vastly different from the great open plains where weather could be seen coming from tens of miles away. While on the ship, some learned to set bearings across such a big sky, but even they found it hard to determine how close the menacing storm loomed. Captain Elias and his riders were the only ones familiar with the storms of big sky country, how fast they could move, how vulnerable the wagons were on the open plain. They rousted the settlers to break camp and start back on the trail with the hope-filled promise of outrunning the storm.

By midmorning, the sky above was fully overcast and the air itself had become enchanted, thick and heavy, making everything, the horses, the wagons, the settlers themselves, appear dreamlike. The mountainous wall of rain had widened and grown taller, so that the wagons and their teams appeared to be mere toys at its edge.

As the day moved on, the clouds above joined into a dense, dark, looming mass that flickered with lightning and rumbled with thunder. Elias rode with one eye on the angry sky and the other on the wagons and the men, women, and children walking beside them.

In an instant, the still in the air was replaced with a hot, humid wind. It first came as a gust but persisted. The white canvases covering the wagons ruffled loudly as they came to life, hats and bonnets flew from those who failed to throw a hand to their heads, and the horses whinnied and shuffled their hooves, making them uneasy to drive.

At a point in the distance between the wall of rain and the wagon train, a black, swirling finger of cloud poked down from the mammoth shelf.

"Tornado," Elias said to himself as the funnel formed and descended to the plain. "Get them to unhitch the horses!" he yelled to his riders. "They're going to run and take the wagons with 'em!"

His men responded, riding the length of the wagon train and issuing his command.

The winds of the widening funnel pressed hard against the plain so that the tall grasses before it became a rolling ocean of waves. Screaming orders over the thunderous roar, Elias and his men helped the pioneers as they franticly struggled to release their teams and to line their tented schooners up with the direction of the wind. Befuddled and confused, they did as they were told. Masters of the ox and plow, the farmers were helpless to the ways of the horse and the open plains. They didn't understand why their teams were let loose, they didn't understand why they were being ordered to lay flat in the grass, and most of all, they didn't understand the wide black funnel moving toward them.

Elias pushed his horse back up the train, inspecting the progress of the settlers. All were free of their teams and down in the high grass—except for one woman. Her husband drowned in the river crossing, leaving her alone to drive their wagon. Elias rushed to assist her in her fight to unhitch her two-horse team. He dismounted his horse and sent it running then cut the caught line holding the team. Free of the wagon, the horses fled in full gallop.

"Get down into the grass," he yelled at three small children still in the tented wagon, and when they didn't respond, he helped the woman to grab each one and lower them to the ground. Then Elias grabbed the woman by her shoulders and pulled her down to the ground with him.

The funnel was upon them.

Elias buried his head into the thick grass, hands pressed to either side. The ground shook beneath him as the roar of a hundred screaming steam engines penetrated through his hands.

He slowly turned his head to the side in time to catch the swirling black cloud lift a wagon at the tail of the train up into the air. The tented canvas ripped away in tatters and the crates the wagon held flew up and away from the wooden box and frame which, free of its load, disintegrated into small pieces of flying, shredded lumber.

A crazed tan horse galloped past Elias directly toward the funnel. The old soldier cringed as the animal was magically lifted and hurled, kicking and neighing, around the twister, and the bottom of the old soldier's chest fell out when the flailing silhouette of one of the settlers followed the pony up into the spin.

With cracks and crackles, the next wagon flew up and exploded a few yards from the ground, followed by a third wagon and another settler.

Then from the base of the twisting black funnel they came: a company of phantom forms, ghastly riders upon horned demon steeds as dark as the swirling cloud they rode from and larger than the wagons of the train.

Elias squinted in disbelief as they charged forth.

They were tall, willowy, and somewhat transparent, their thin faces and those of the beasts they rode were without feature except for the bright, burning yellow of their eyes. They whooped and hollered as they charged, whipping their mounts to a fury, seemingly pulling the screaming funnel close behind them, as if they were the stormbringers incarnate.

A thunderous roar from above cut into Elias's skull.

He rolled to his back in frantic pain, and in horror witnessed the huge indigo shelf cloud high above take the form of a massive wings. For a brief moment, Elias thought of the mighty bird the young Comanche guide had spoken of, but before his thoughts could fully form, the mass of black ink beneath the wings morphed into the shape of a gargantuan creature. A bolt of fear went through him as he gazed upward at the wide torso, shoulders, and arms of the winged cloud beast emerging from of the expansive swirling funnel of wind and rain.

A dark blip of a demon rider in the corner of Elias's eye caused him to spin his head in time witness those riding nearest the wagons as they attacked those hiding in the grass. The demons appeared to swing long handled hooks down into the grassy plain, striking the defenseless settlers hiding there, launching them up into the strong wind where they took flight.

He watched the marauding company of demons charge forward, indiscriminately assailing whomever they came upon. But as his weary, glazed eyes focused, he realized that the long weapons were the tendril arms of the riders themselves, extending eight to ten feet from their shoulders.

Then from behind them, the huge wisping forearm of the indigo cloud giant swung down, striking a wagon, sending it shattered into the air.

Elias rolled and threw himself across the woman and her children beside him to shield them from the oncoming onslaught.

The acrid smell of sulphur preceded the rider's approach, burrowing deep up into Elias's sinuses, burning the insides of his cheeks, further watering his eyes.

Prepared to be struck by one of the long-hooked tendrils, Elias braced himself and pulled his revolver from its holster. But as the first of the riders rode past, they chose not to strike.

Then one slowed and stopped above him.

Elias put both hands to his revolver and pointed it up towards the creature's head.

The demon gazed down and fixed its burning yellow eyes on Elias and the woman and children beneath and beside him. The creature was neither man nor beast, its eyes indeed yellow burning flames, deep, hollow, and unforgiving. An empty ache of longing and loneliness washed over Elias as he faced his end. Frozen, motionless in the maelstrom of wind, rain, debris, and sadness, the barrel of his gun dropped down.

The demon stared down for less than a few seconds, but to Elias it seemed an eternity. Then, without word or signal, the demon rider reared his steed back onto its two hind legs. Long black and shiny claws, as thick and sharp as a grizzly's, protruded from the demon steed's huge paws; its nostrils flared, snorting wisps of black smoke that rose and curled around the creature's horns.

Facing his fear, Elias raised the barrel of his gun again.

But the rider appeared unfazed.

From the front of the wagon train came the boom of a rifle, then another. The creature jetted his attention forward.

Elias turned to discover Elden, the Comanche guide, out on the plain away from the wagons, waving his arms, firing a rifle up into the air. The demon whipped his steed's hind quarter with the tip of his tendril arm, and with a bellow barely heard above the screaming funnel, the steed launched forward and away from Elias.

Elias never fired.

He watched as other demon riders rode past, then shielded himself and the others beside him as the black funnel skirted the wagon train, following the riders' path.

The wagon beside him rocked, the canvas tore back from the front ribbing securing it, and the two wheels on the side of Elias and the funnel lifted.

Then the funnel passed, and the wagon set back down to rest.

A dense rain followed, soaking the prairie, blinding Elias, and when it had passed, the funnel and the riders that had accompanied it were gone.

The dark blanket of sky above separated into clouds that in turn parted away from each other to let in the bright blue of day and the golden rays of the sun, shining down on what was left of the settlers' party and the remnants of destruction.

Mustering what sense of it all that he could, Elias sat up, then rose to his feet. He helped the woman up, and the children as well. Then he inspected the field.

The old soldier had lived through battles won and lost. And as different as this was, the result was no different at all. The pungent stench of sulfur hung in the air, wrought by the demons rather than the exploding gunpowder of the war—but the smell was the same. As was the blood, the dismemberments, and the debris that stretched across the grassy plain in every direction.

As he had as a Captain in battle, old Elias pondered prayer, again sought to make sense of the senseless, but as in the past, there was no sense to it all that he could determine. Then upon seeing Randall and the other survivors rise from the field, he focused on what needed to be done: to rally the survivors to pick up the pieces, salvage what could be salvaged, and to lead the wagon train further along the Oregon Trail.

In the days that followed, he didn't speak of the demon riders, and if any had seen what he had, they didn't speak of it either. Even when Elden rejoined the wagon train with the cattle and horses that had scurried from the train, nothing was said.

ABOUT THE AUTHORS

Robert Jeschonek – According to Mike Resnick, Robert Jeschonek "is a towering talent." Robert is an award-winning writer whose fiction, comics, essays, articles, and podcasts have been published around the world. His young adult fantasy novel, *My Favorite Band Does Not Exist*, won the Forward National Literature Award and was named one of BOOKLIST's Top Ten First Novels for Youth. His cross-genre science fiction thriller, *Day 9*, is an International Book Award winner. He also won the 2013 Scribe Award for Best Original Novel from the International Association of Media Tie-in Writers for his alternate history, *TANNHÄUSER: RISING SUN, FALLING SHADOWS*. Simon & Schuster, DAW/Penguin Books, and DC Comics have published his work. He won the grand prize in Pocket Books' nationwide Strange New Worlds contest and was nominated for the British Fantasy Award. Visit him online at www.thefictioneer.com. You can also find him on Facebook and follow him as @TheFictioneer on Twitter.

Steven Van Patten is from Fort Greene, Brooklyn. After graduating from Long Island University on a full-tuition scholarship, he pursued a career in television production. After paying his dues, Steven went on to stage manage a plethora of TV shows, most recently *The Mel Robbins Show* and *The View*, all the while dreaming up his macabre tales. The storyline of his first novel was born from watching horror movies as a child and noticing a lack of diversity, and character development when people of color were employed. After pouring over historical research night after night, and traveling alone to various locales, including Senegal, West Africa and Osaka, Japan, he wrote the first three installments of the **Brookwater's Curse** horror novel series, which featured a 1860s Georgia plantation slave who becomes a vampire.

After receiving much praise, several glowing reviews from various book club heavy hitters, and literary awards for each book, Steven was admitted into the Horror Writer's Association. His next two novels, **'Killer Genius: She Kills Because She Cares'** and **'Killer Genius 2: Attack of The Gym Rats'**—pitted a hyper-intelligent, socially conscious female serial killer against a well-intentioned African-American detective. It debuted at NYC Comic Con in October of 2015 and was nominated for an *African-American Literary Show Award* for Best Mystery/ Suspense in 2016. Three years later, **'Hell At The Way Station'**, Steven's collaboration with Marc Abbott, a horror anthology with a sort of Arabian Knights twist, won Best Anthology and Best In Sci-Free.

Visit Steven at his website brookwaterscurse.com

Steve Oden has worked in the publishing industry–mainly newspapers and magazines–for more than 30 years. Although retired, he provides editorial services on a consulting basis, mainly to corporate clients, and writes on assignment. His newspaper columns have appeared regularly in Tennessee and Alabama publications since 1980, winning awards from the Alabama Press Association, University of Tennessee-Tennessee Press Association, Society of Professional Journalists, National Rural Electric Cooperative Association and several wildlife conservation organizations.

Teel James Glenn was born in Brooklyn and has traveled the world for thirty years as a Stuntman/ Fight choreographer/ Swordmaster, Jouster, Book Illustrator, Storyteller, Bodyguard and Actor (Yes he was Vega in Streetfighter: the later Years). And has done over 80 films and 55 Renaissance Faires in most of the above capacities.
He's had stories and articles printed in scores of magazines from *AfterburnSF*, *Classic Pulp Fiction stories*, *Blazing Adventures*, *Weird Tales*, and *Mad to Black Belt and Fantasy Tales* and a number of books published.
You can keep up with his new adventures at theurbanswashbuckler.com

Hunter C. Eden is a Denver-based essayist and dark fantasy writer whose work has appeared in *Weird Tales, City Slab*, and *Ravenous Monster Horror Webzine*.

Jessica West (a.k.a. West1Jess) is currently pursuing a state of self-induced psychosis, also known as writing. In the past, she has worked for Wal-Mart, a lawyer, and a bank. Now if she could just get a couple years experience with the IRS and the NSA, world domination is in the bag.

Jess lives in Acadiana with three daughters still young enough to think she's cool and a husband who knows better but likes her anyway.

Daniel Arthur Smith is a USA Today bestselling author. His titles include *Spectral Shift*, *Hugh Howey Lives*, *The Cathari Treasure*, *The Somali Deception*, and a few other novels and short stories. He also curates the phenomenal short fiction series *Tales from the Canyons of the Damned* and *Frontiers of Speculative Fiction*.

He was raised in Michigan and graduated from Western Michigan University where he studied philosophy, with focus on cognitive science, meta-physics, and comparative religion. He began his career as a bartender, barista, poetry house proprietor, teacher, and then became a technologist and futurist for the Fortune 100 across the Americas and Europe.

Daniel has traveled to over 300 cities in 22 countries, residing in Los Angeles, Kalamazoo, Prague, Crete, and now writes in Manhattan where he lives with his wife and young sons.

For news and updates visit danielarthursmith.com